SECRET

Rabbi Gabrielle Series, Novel 7

Roger E. Herst

Dale Hill Publishing

Contents

Chapter One

0600 hours.

Itamar Arad, Director of Israel Antiquities, normally avoided his secured text messaging, using it only when absolutely essential. When such a message arrived on his phone at Kibbutz Ha-on on the Golan Heights overlooking the Sea of Galilee he sensed bad news. While subjecting it to his phone-specific encryption he took a deep breath before expelling the air through his lips with a faint whistle. The message bore the signature of Porcupine, his contact in Israel's Secret Service, Mossad. Porcupine was an icy cold man whom Itamar believed to be the last person on the planet he would voluntarily choose as a friend. Equally, Porcupine made no attempt to camouflage his contempt for academics; people like Itamar who were frequently and involuntarily attached to his unit. Whether or not these intellectuals were dreamy *Luftmenchen* divorced from reality or cold pragmatists that Mossad required to conduct its business, Porcupine was diplomatic enough to withhold from public judgment.

Report to PM's Jerusalem office ASAP! See attached YouTube entry

Itamar read the message twice to be certain he understood. Next, he booted his computer to the YouTube page and viewed a particular fragment from the illegal diggings at Qumran that he and his lover Gabby Lewyn had turned over to the safe-keeping of the previous Prime Minister, Ezra Rahav. Rahav had subsequently suffered a heart attack in office and was succeeded by Vice-Prime Minister Zebulon Sonnenberg. At the time, Itamar and Gabby were required to sign a gag order to disclose nothing of this fragment. From that moment forth Itamar had put this speck of parchment out of mind, focusing his attentions on multiple and often contradictory demands as Israel's Director of Antiquities. In the subsequent minutes on the Golan Heights his mind flooded with 14 month old memories—the transfer of the document, dubbed "Yeshu" to the then Prime Minister Rahav, the following negotiations with Donaldo Cardinal Fornenti in the Vatican, followed by an exchange of supplementary Qumran fragments from Rome to Israel. How this previously secret business had leaked to the Internet he had no idea, only that as one of the select few aware of the *Yeshu* Fragment he knew for certain he was not the leaker. And if he were not culpable, it was probably Gabby Lewyn! While he would vouch from her honesty to keep her word, he could also conjure up a scenario in which she would enjoy a heated squabble with the Church of Rome.

But for the moment this was not his primary concern. Israel military command on the border with Syria was scheduled to inform him at 0730 hours where and when they intended to open the security fence and admit selected casualties from the bloody conflict in Syria for emergency medical attention. Among these wounded fighters he expected Kar'ine Salik, a Muslim originally from Syria with whom he had worked so successfully on his previous assignment the Muslim world. In Istanbul the Israeli agents had promised Kar'ine sanctuary in Israel, but later withdrew their pledge saying it was all a misunderstanding. *Mumzarim* (bastards) that Itamar knew them to be, their broken word didn't deter them from re-offering her Israeli domicile for additional favors, and extremely life-threatening dangerous ones at that.

Kar'ine Salik had been scheduled to cross at Checkpoint *Yedidut* into the Israeli Golan Heights during a previous week, but without explanation did not show up. The standing plan was that should the original crossing fail at the appointed time, a second effort would be made exactly a week later. Since she failed to show up on schedule the second week Itamar was more than worried. Waiting for her third and perhaps last attempt drained him. He found it impossible to concentrate on anything but Kar'ine. Though she was quintessentially Syrian and spoke native Syrian Arabic, gathering intelligence for Israel was a life-threatening enterprise. During the week Itamar pledged that once she had safely crossed into Israel he would never permit her to go back to her home country, no matter the compelling circumstances.

The order from the newly elected prime minister, Zebulon Sonnenberg, produced an impossible conflict for Itamar. During the crossing from Syria he was required to personally identify Kar'ine and sign a temporary visa. Without this signature it was possible the Israeli Army (IDF) would return her to Syria. If she survived there, it might take months to organize a new crossing.

A quick calculation told Itamar that there was a single alternative. He thereupon dashed for his Toyota to race eastward along *Rehov* 98 to the frontier checkpoint where, if he could stir a sympathetic IDF officer, he might leave a signature for Kar'ine's visa and his secured phone number to call when she arrived. Then it would take a high-speed drive back to Jerusalem, conduct whatever business the Prime Minister had in mind, and barrel back to the Syrian checkpoint, in time. He detested time-conflicts, but what alternative had he?

* * * * *

Gabrielle Lewyn, now 38 years old, lost patience for Itamar's frequent disappearances. When she reviewed the chronology of their relationship, she realized that he was absent from her life most of the time. As Director of Antiquities a certain amount of absence was to be expected, but what they enjoyed as a couple was hardly satisfying. He always had an excuse and, more often than not, it was on a confidential matter for the government that couldn't be shared. To make matters worse, he wouldn't, or more probably couldn't, tell her where he was going.

Gabby had believed much of that would change when they returned to Jerusalem from the West Bank, where Itamar's sabbatical duties with the Palestine Historical and Cultural Society ended and he resumed his previous office as director. Nothing could have been further from the truth. In fact, upon his return he was more secretive than ever, gone from their home in Talpiot district frequently and less physically intimate. She marshaled her powers to understand the changes that had come over him but came up with little. Years practicing as a rabbi in the States had taught her to be wary of blissful marriages, or in her own case, blissful relationships. They were always a work in progress, each party learning daily to cope with the non-Hollywood version of matrimonial bliss.

* * * * *

Work was Gabby's prescription for her ailments; deflecting from her own problems to fixing those of others.

Her appointment as Special American Negotiator to promote her rental plan for the Two-State Solution to the Israeli-Palestinian imbroglio had failed to gather traction. Political pundits who had made their careers analyzing Israel-Arab relations declared it *Dead on Arrival.* But the US State Department, which had a penchant for inventing self-serving slogans, claimed her diplomacy had not failed, but had simply gone into a *period of dormancy.* Gabby's Rental Plan had never followed a neat progression from conflict to resolution. Palestinians and Jewish negotiators brought to the table 90 years of mutual mistrust, compounded by an ongoing history of violence that daily established another layer of mistrust. No easy formula for Gabby to overcome. The hiatus in her diplomatic efforts meant that she had time for a video documentary she was writing on the archeological discoveries of her deceased boyfriend, Professor Timothy Matternly from the University of Chicago. To this end, a new collaboration had been formed with Lydia Browner, who once was Gabby's tennis coach in Washington DC but who in subsequent years had reinvented herself as director of a video production company. Warpath Productions was currently on location at Sodom, bordering the Dead Sea, preparing to shoot a documentary about Tim Matternly in the Judean Desert. Gabby remained in Jerusalem, working from an office in The Shrine of the Book, where the museum's special wing displayed parchment fragments from Qumran's Cave XII unearthed by Timothy Matternly.

This morning there was an air of expectancy in the lobby of the Shrine's office complex. Something didn't feel right, but something Gabby couldn't immediately identify. A napping guard was seated in the foyer, dreaming of events elsewhere. Somewhat unusual, no one was waiting for the elevator when it appeared on the ground floor. The long hallway threading between offices of the museum's administrative staff was also vacant. She fished in her Turkish leather purse for a key to unlock what suddenly appeared to be open. An unnerving presentiment from the lobby returned when she discovered no resistance from the door.

Immediately standing from a conference chair beside her desk a middle-aged man with a completely shaven head and wearing an expensive Italian designed leather jacket turned to greet her. Offering a hand to shake, he introduced himself as Yair Lifkovitz from Israel's Knesset Police. Having been seated in her own chair behind the desk, a second man, this one heavyset with a thin silver beard and a bulky double-chin, jumped up and swished around the desk to introduce himself as Detective Sergeant Joram Oz.

"I guess I don't need an introduction. You obviously know who I am," Gabby snapped, struggling with a surging sense of alarm. "I'm not sure I understand why you've let yourselves into my office. Mind telling me?"

"The Prime Minister wants to see you. We've come to escort you to his office."

A year and two months before she had business with the then Deputy-Prime Minister Zebulon Sonnenberg. Since then, not a word had passed between them, though in national elections after Ezra Rahav's death she had favored the Labor Party, knowing that were it to be successful, Sonnenberg was first on the party list and would become the elected prime minister.

"What's he want to see me for?" she barely camouflaged her anxiety. Both government agents flicked their heads in a gesture to convey that they were not permitted to answer. "Does the PM have a date in mind?"

"I said we've come to escort you. Not to arrange an appointment," growled Yair Lifkovitz.

"Suppose I cannot make it just now?"

"Then we'll wait until you can. When you're ready I'll call the PM's office to let him know we're on the way."

"I have a staff meeting in an hour."

Oz took a step toward Gabby, almost a hostile movement, before holding back. "I'm afraid you cannot speak with anyone at this moment. Not because we say so, but because we have orders from the PM."

"Suppose he doesn't have time for me?"

"He'll make it," barked Lifkovitz.

Acknowledging to herself that in the past she had a pleasant and mutually satisfying relationship with Sonnenberg there was no reason to be apprehensive. Moreover it didn't look as if she had any alternatives.

* * * * *

While being ushered from the museum building by government agents she hoped to avoid colleagues. A blue-black limousine awaited them for a short ride from the Shrine of the Book to the Office of the Prime Minister.

In Sonnenberg's office Gabby confronted a surprise that eclipsed her exasperation at having been shanghaied by government officials. Standing beside the PM's desk was Itamar Arad in a bleached white shirt and equally well-starched khaki pants. He pivoted from a courtyard window and for an instant seemed equally surprised to find her also present in Israel's most important office. Gabby stepped forward to embrace him. During an awkward moment he hesitated returning her warmth, but eventually wrapped his arms around her. Her lips traversed his neck and ran along the stubble of his thin, fashionable beard but did not move farther toward his mouth. When they separated she said, "It takes a prime minister to bring you home these days."

His mind jumped to the frontier with Syria while glancing down at his Apple watch to calculate when Kar'ine Salik was expected to cross.

"Know why the PM has brought us together?" she inquired.

"He hasn't told me. Surely, he's got something in his bonnet."

Conversation eased into a rapid series of meaningless questions about health and Puccini, the feral cat that Itamar had rescued from neighborhood streets and which Gabby cared for during his frequent business trips.

Prime Minister Sonnenberg was not immediately available. Gabby and Itamar waited on a Swedish sofa. A knock-your-socks-off beautiful Yemenite secretary, reminding Gabby of her Baha'i girlfriend Farryda Sorrel, popped in to the waiting room to offer *mitz*, fruit juice, which both refused. While waiting, Gabby surmised that the urgency of this meeting was probably related to something she had done while functioning as an American negotiator during the last peace discussions with the Palestinians. Israeli officials were always skeptical of American motives when dealing with Arabs. During the meetings she knew that Israeli agents were fundamentally hostile to her Rental Scheme. In contrast Palestinian negotiators were refreshingly open. Of course, she was not naïve. In her plan Israelis had far more to lose than Palestinians. In the simplest terms, if her Rental Scheme produced results Palestinians would acquire their desired sovereignty at the expense of security for the Jewish state.

With no forewarning the office door swung open and Zebulon Sonnenberg plowed through like a giant reaping machine, accompanied by three aids. No longer the sprite, irreverent, foul-speaking deputy prime minister they once knew, but an aged, overweight and over-burdened governor of what many Israelis believed to be the most un-governable nation on the planet. Fourteen months before he had been extremely friendly with Itamar and Gabby, perhaps believing them to be loyal servants—one a hard-nosed academic type well suited to policing Israel's archeological treasures, and the other, an iconoclastic, liberal female rabbi, unpolluted by living too long in the cesspool of Israeli politics. At the time Sonnenberg was remarkably unfiltered and refreshingly unlike the sycophants surrounding him. That forthright quality allowed them to be frank in his presence.

But Sonnenberg had obviously changed. He barely mounted a hello; instead limping as a man with back problems to his desk. With the back of his hand he whisked away his advisors, a well-practiced signal for them to leave. As they were moving toward the door the old man dropped into his chair and without a word of greeting began punching a computer keyboard. Gabby noticed that there was little dexterity in his heavy fingers and he was forced to delete and retype many of the commands.

"Iti," he ignored Gabby and addressed his antiquities director without looking up, "you must have seen this on YouTube," then twirled the screen before their eyes. Finally acknowledging Gabby as a member of the conversation, he said, "And you, Rabbi?"

She had to lean over the desk in an ungraceful angle that exposed a shallow cleavage below her blouse, which she had often remarked to intimates, "had become far less enticing with the passage of years." She didn't believe an old *alta-cocker* like the PM would be interested, though she noted his eyes momentarily lingered on the edge of her blouse. And then in the first moment of warmth, he cocked his head to gaze upon her eyes as she read the screen. "Have you people seen this?" he asked in a gravelly voice.

Three words! The first consisting of three Aramaic letters in the ancient script of the Dead Sea Scrolls. Gabby's blood seemed to depart her extremities and flood the region of her heart. Her voice faltered for an embarrassing moment. "No …why, no I haven't. Iti, have you?" A nod of his head acknowledged that he had been ordered to look at it just before coming to Jerusalem.

"You recognize this, of course?" growled Sonnenberg.

Both did. The three Aramaic letters Y, SH, U spelled Yeshu, the name of the Preacher Jesus from Nazareth who eventually became deified by the Church of Rome to become the second member of Christianity's holy trio: The Father, **the Son**, and the Holy Ghost. *Yeshu* was further identified as bar Yosef, the son of Joseph. She knew Sonnenberg appreciated the significance of these letters spelling the name of the Christian Savior, particularly because it was contemporaneous with other Dead Sea fragments written at the dawn of the First Century when the man Jesus, not yet known as Deity Jesus, was purported to have lived. Never, never before in the entire history of Christianity had his name been mentioned *while* he was alive. The earliest subsequent recordings of the name *Yeshu*, the son of Joseph, were found in the Gospels, no earlier than 40-50 years *after* the Preacher's death, a full generation later!

What made this fragment so controversial was not its existence, but where it was discovered. The *Yeshu* Fragment, according to Professor Tim Matternly, was found in Qumran, along with the names of other students from a remote desert school farther south. And what was so significant about this school was that there dedicated students trained themselves to become spokesmen for God. This meant that prophecy was not bestowed by Deity but learned and practiced by eager students. And there was textual evidence to believe that the young Jesus had been a member of this student body.

Gabby had originally found the *Yeshu* Fragment hidden by Tim Matternly in the Jerusalem apartment they then shared. Tucked into a Kittel Bible, a scholarly Hebrew edition of the Old Testament Masoretic text, she knew it to be the legal property of the State of Israel, according to a well-established law designating all archeological artifacts not already in private hands to belong to the state. This astounding piece of parchment was immediately delivered to the then Prime Minister Ezra Raviv and his deputy Zebulon Sonnenberg. The *Yeshu* fragment was so explosive Gabby and Itamar were forced to sign an unconditional gag order to reveal nothing of its existence. In a gentleman's agreement between themselves they refrained from speaking about it. For fourteen months the fragment remained out-of-sight, out-of-mind.

"On YouTube!" she sounded her surprise to the PM. "Who would post a thing like this on the Internet?"

"That's what I want to know. I've known Iti throughout his career. But you, Rabbi, you're different and you're my chief suspect."

Gabby studied the image more carefully. Across Sonnenberg's desk the fragment was small and hard to discern. She would have wanted to study it on her computer in order to enlarge the image and compare the shape and color. Itamar had temporarily stored the original fragment in the Ministry's safe for security. In exchange for the single *Yeshu* Fragment the Church of Rome returned less valuable Dead Sea documents that eventually found a home in the Matternly Wing of the Shrine of the Book.

Gabby and Itamar also pledged that no copies of the fragment had ever been made in any format. That was an essential part of the deal between Israel and Donaldo Cardinal Fornenti, the Pope's senior executive. Absolutely no copies. Gabby had signed but also cheated. Early in the process well before negotiations with the Vatican and even before she delivered the fragment to Itamar, she had made a single photocopy and carefully hid it in a *daf* (page) of the Talmud, Tractate *Terumot*, in the Judaica portion of her home library. She had scrupulously avoided looking at it. Now suddenly out of the blue, it was front and center, and likely to cause a firestorm that would eventually suck her in.

"Any idea who posted this?" she asked Sonnenberg.

"I told you, you're my chief suspect. I can never trust you Americans. You dance to your own music and write rules as you go."

Gabby disguised umbrage, "You've got a herd of smart-as-hell tech people in this office. Surely they can figure out who posted this."

"I can employ all the computer nerds I want, but that's certain to spread this secret and give Israel a black eye. Why do that when I have the culprit in front of me?"

She raised her voice, failing to conceal the affront. "You would never have learned about this fragment if I hadn't brought it to Itamar's attention. I have no idea who's behind this, but certainly not me. Perhaps somebody in the Vatican." It then occurred to her that before jumping to conclusions it would be best to compare her private photocopy. Many deceptions appeared on YouTube. This could be a fake having nothing to do with Tim Matternly's discovery at Qumran.

She was comfortable that if government agents expropriated her home computer they would never think to search her library, particularly her Talmudic books. But at the moment there was no way to get home. No one, absolutely no one, knew about the photocopy. And as far as she was concerned, it was going to remain that way.

The PM resumed, "Young lady, you can imagine our dicey relations with Rome. Churchmen have never liked Jews from day one. They go out of their way to favor the Palestinians. The Holy See suffers Israel only because we control many of its sacred sites. Their people in the Vatican must have noticed this YouTube entry." Gabby shook her head. She sensed Sonnenberg was baiting her. "And you know what the Pope will do? His august lieutenants will say the YouTube fragment is a fake. Scholars, who have never seen it, will climb aboard. How hard will it be to deny what never officially existed?"

That sounded reasonable to Gabby. Perhaps the PM was making a mountain from a molehill. If the Vatican declared the YouTube entry a phony, no one would be the wiser. End of problem.

"And then what do you think will happen?" the PM looked to Itamar.

"Not sure, sir," he sounded sheepish, a characteristic uncommon for one who was never shy about wielding the full authority of his office.

"Well, I'll tell you. The media will be all over both of you. You are the go-to authorities on the discoveries of Dr. Matternly. And you, Rabbi, have written more on them than anyone. I'm told that you have a film crew working at the Dead Sea as we speak. The media will look to you for confirmation of the Vatican's denial."

That possibility had not entered her mind.

"So you two have your work cut out," Sonnenberg said.

"How so?" Itamar shot back.

"Tomorrow afternoon there will be a press conference in which you will announce this YouTube posting to be as phony as the Piltdown

Man. We must beat the Vatican to declaring it a fake so that Church-men will know Israel keeps its word. This issue must disappear! And the sooner the better."

She caught Itamar in a moment of distraction before saying, "As Director of Antiquities you should make the announcement. Not me."

He rushed back to the conversation. "On this issue, you're far better known. More articles, more speeches. You're the living memory of Tim Matternly's work."

"But what if it isn't fake?" Gabby redirected toward the Prime Minister, a slight tremor in her voice. "We all know it could be the real McCoy."

Sonnenberg was ready with a response. "Of course. But that would mean Israel had breached its agreement with Rome. And I'm not willing to do that. Our word must remain sacred. We do what we say we will. That's the beginning, the middle and the end."

"And lie about the veracity of the fragment?"

"We don't know for certain it's genuine, but if it is, it's a private lie between willing partners. The Vatican and the State of Israel agree on very little, these days."

"And if I refuse to participate in this falsehood and set the historical understanding of Jesus back another thousand years, what then?"

Sonnenberg sighed as though he had not fully considered the matter. Eventually, he said, "We prosecute you, Rabbi Lewyn, for violating a host of laws breaching state security. You'll spend much of your budding career fighting the government, and all of your life-long savings for lawyers. I don't think you'd appreciate the hospitality of our prisons. Hard to imagine you'd want to follow that route for a mere fragment of parchment with the name of a man whose devout follow-ers have cause Jews so much suffering."

Gabby felt blood evacuating her face as a twitch ran from her spine along the Sciatic nerve. She didn't believe old Sonnenberg would really do that because it would eventually sweep him into a conspiracy. But it was nevertheless a sobering threat. In that moment she knew what Sonnenberg didn't – that there was a way for her to compare the YouTube entry with the real thing. If it proved to be a hoax, there was no reason not to add her authority to that of the Vatican. But on the other hand, should it prove to be genuine, that was another matter. Would she really want to add her name to an outrageous falsehood, especially when the implication for modern Christians struggling with their faith was so significant?

"Time is of the essence here," said the Prime Minister. "It will please the Vatican to see that Israel has been quick to condemn this fraud. The media will not follow a hoax for long."

She shot back, "If neither I nor Itamar leaked this, the culprit must be in Rome."

"Pope Francis runs a tight ship. For all I know He sleeps with this fragment under his pillow. And that's the way I want it to continue. I'm not a betting man, but all my instincts tell me that you, Rabbi, are the leaker. Based on what my spies tell me, you'd like nothing more than to get into a theological scrap about the divinity of Jesus. But what you don't understand, friend, is that in the long run it doesn't matter what our fragment proves. The Church has created its place in history around the Trinity. Nothing will change just because we learn that a fellow by the name of Jesus happened to be a student in a desert school where they trained young men to become spokesmen for God."

Keeping focused on Sonnenberg's argument proved difficult when Gabby's mind was now flooded with reservations.

Dials on the PM's phone lit up and several odd sounds on his computer signaled email was being received. Itamar and Gabby sensed that the meeting was coming to an end. This was confirmed when he said, "I'm going to give you until tomorrow afternoon to prepare your denials. My people will immediately disseminate what you say in the media."

Itamar's brain was flooding. Of course, he would have to obey the Prime Minister's wish, which he calculated provided about 17 hours, in which time he could rush back to the Golan Heights and hopefully received Kar'ine among the Syrian casualties.

Gabby's thoughts were elsewhere. She was acutely aware she had not agreed to this government manipulation. But if, as she hoped, the *Yeshu* fragment proved fraudulent, there was no reason not to cooperate. The whole affair, as Sonnenberg correctly pointed out, might rapidly blow over.

It turned out that the old man was full of surprises, complicating her return to the Talpiot home. Until the press conference, he wanted Itamar and her to remain nearby and work with his staff.

A government marshal, a wiry, stern-looking official in a wrinkled khaki uniform, escorted them to furnished apartments maintained for VIPs doing business with Cabinet officials. A well-furnished two-bedroom suite with an Italian leather sofa and crimson leather twirling chairs was situated on the second floor.

"It's been stocked with food for you guys," the marshal said in an upbeat tone, as though he were delivering a valuable amenity. "There's a gym in the basement. The master bedroom closet has workout clothes. I'll be hanging out in the lobby so just let me know what you need. The PM wants you back in his office tomorrow at two p.m. sharp. Understand?"

No, she really didn't, but perhaps she wasn't meant to. To be confined was the last thing she wanted and would require her to sneak away before the press conference. Adding to her trouble, the apartment was on the second floor making it impossible to escape through a window.

* * * * *

Itamar entered the vestibule of the government VIP apartment and reluctantly followed Gabby as far as the bedroom door before stopping. A glance at his watch told him that if he were to meet the Prime Minister's schedule he must leave for the Golan immediately.

Gabby stepped from the window to embrace him, probing to determine whether their previous absence had instilled a physical desire to take advantage of the king-sized bed. It was immediately clear that he lacked interest, almost to the point of pushing her away. "I've got an important engagement that I can't miss," he said in a nervous voice. "I'll be back in time to make the press conference."

Feeling rejected, Gabby back-stepped to the bed and dropped onto the white spread. "Are you comfortable doing Sonnenberg his dirty business?"

"Have I an alternative? The old man's my boss, and there are dozens of competitors in the field who would love my job. We're not talking archeology or even Christian theology. Gabb, this is about putting bread on the table."

"Well, I'm not comfy with the idea. If the fragment is a fraud, that's one thing. But if it turns out differently, how can I go public and confirm an outright lie? If and when the truth eventually comes out, there goes my reputation. And then I'm in your camp, Iti. For me, it's not just about historical truth; it's also about career."

Itamar growled impatience. "I haven't got time to argue this now. We'll talk when I return. I suggest you follow me into the press conference with an enthusiastic denial. Anything less will produce consequences you're not going to like."

Gabby felt herself teetering on a fence. Itamar was correct: if the YouTube fragment was a fake she should denounce it. But Itamar didn't know about her photocopy. And if it proved the fragment was authentic, everything was different. While she had hoped there would be some physical intimacy with Itamar, she was also happy that he would be occupied for several hours, time for her to return home and check the photocopy stashed in her volume of *Terumot*.

She followed him as he withdrew to the entry door, tugging his arm to turn and acknowledge as she attempted to plant a kiss upon his cheek. He dipped his face to receive her lips and was slightly off-balance. "I'm scared, Iti. This business is bigger than you or me. And we're going to get sucked into a mix-master whether we like it or not. I don't believe it will blow over as the Prime Minister said. It's bigger than Zebulon Sonnenberg or the Holy Father in Rome. We're overturning Christian history and I don't believe millions of Christians will like what they have been taught in their catechisms."

Itamar pulled himself free. "No time for this, Gabb. I'll let you wrestle with the implications; for the moment I have other needs."

"Of course," she replied, knowing what neither Itamar nor the Prime Minister could possibly know about the photocopy.

Route 98. North of the Quneitra Overlook
on the Golan Heights

The Israeli Army had established a military off-limits zone, five kilometers from the frontier with Syria. There was no barbed wire, perhaps because it would do nothing to stop Syrian armored vehicles attacking from the east. But the Army had posted the zone against trespassers and probably planted mines alongside a dirt track leading to the *Yedidut* checkpoint. An unarmed civilian such as Itamar was seldom granted the privilege of approaching the frontier. But Itamar's credentials convinced two military guards he had a right to proceed.

He arrived in a compound surrounded by a series of barbed wire fences, each with a gate manned by armed soldiers. On this morning, the deputy commander, Major Shai Makket was supervising the passage of seventeen wounded Syrian soldiers, preselected for humanitarian and public relations reasons on the other side of the frontier for eventual transit into Israel. Itamar could see in the distance a gaggle of Syrian military ambulances and what appeared to be a cluster of hospital gurneys ready to be wheeled into No Man's Land separating hostile armies.

The major appeared nervous as he marched among young Israeli soldiers, unnecessarily barking orders and often returning to an officer he had previously spoken with. Having witnessed this process twice before while waiting for Kar'ine, Itamar was familiar with the procedure. First came Israeli *Mogan Dovid* ambulances to disgorge stretchers bearing Syrian soldiers who had completed medical treatment in Israel and were being returned to their native soil. Ambulatory patients able to transit the frontier on crutches without assistance followed. Before crossing each Syrian was processed and photographed on the Israeli side, after which unarmed Israeli soldiers maneuvered stretchers into No Man's Land to join Syrian medics.

The process was slow but thorough. One by one, Syrians who had completed their treatment entered No Man's Land and eventually disappeared into waiting vehicles on the other side. Itamar expected the slow process would reverse itself as a new crop of Syrians casualties waited for transfer into Israel. Knowing that he must first see that Kar'ine was in good hands and then race back to Jerusalem, this methodical procedure did not suit his purpose. For him, her arrival was more a dream than a fact. He had already been disappointed on two occasions.

Israeli soldiers would not permit him to stand by the entry gate and survey each gurney as it was escorted into Israel territory. Rather, he was forced to wait beside a pool of ambulances waiting for a triage team to determine whether a patient went to a First Aid Station just outside Qatzrin or immediately transferred to a full service hospital in Haifa.

One by one he examined the new patients arriving at the triage station in intervals of fifteen minutes. And as each proved to be a gravely wounded soldier, he found his spirits tumbling. After the eleventh patient, Itamar neared despair. If Kar'ine didn't show up on this occasion the chance of her never leaving Syria mounted. He had in mind a Plan B, but if inaugurated it had less than a ten percent chance of success. Kar'ine's demise in Syria was unthinkable. Yes, of course, he would survive. But things would never be the same again. And this, no matter how Gabby might compensate for the loss.

Syrian fighters suffered the horrors of modern warfare, burns mostly from high explosives and shrapnel that pierced their flesh, crunching bone en route to vital organs. Itamar had seen wounded comrades during his military service, but never so many in which the rules of combat had been abandoned. He thought of himself as trained to accept casualties, yet what he witnessed shattered his defenses. The miserable creatures of civil war in Syria momentarily distracted his attention from patients twelve and thirteen, one without legs and the other with only half a face. As they moved forward toward the triage station he questioned the purpose of providing care for men whose lives had been ruined on the battlefield.

Patient fourteen was wheeled into the triage station. Itamar noted a covey of Israelis soldiers clustering around the gurney as it approached. The body, if still alive, was heavily blanketed; a strap over the forehead maintained the skull in a fixed position. Often Arabic speaking Israeli staff asked questions. But on this occasion they must have reckoned the patient was injured beyond speech. Itamar stepped as close as he thought the medical staff would permit.

An officer suddenly emerged from the triage tent, looked around and eventually eyed Itamar. He waved his arm to signal while whistling through his front teeth. A second signal motioned for Itamar to approach for a word. At the identical moment Itamar's cell phone vibrated in his pocket. Out of habit, a hand withdrew the instrument and slapped it against his ear.

A raspy voice snapped in the receiver. "Porcupine here. Iti, she's coming through today. I'm sure you're on the border. Look for her."

"She's not here," he replied.

"Look again. You can't miss a woman. Take her immediately to Kibbutz Ha-on. We'll debrief her tomorrow."

"You can't debrief someone who isn't here. And if you could, I can't make it. I'm under orders from the PM. That's right. Good old Zebulon himself."

An extended pause ensued. "Well, then day after tomorrow. I'll be there are at 1100 hours."

"You can come when you wish, but don't expect to find Kar'ine."

At that moment the medic who had signaled from the triage tent marched over to him and tugged. "A real chic under all those blankets and bandages. I'd say a big improvement over the train wrecks the Syrians usually send us."

Back talking to Porcupine Itamar announced, "They've got a woman here. Could be Kar'ine. Let me check. How did you know she was coming today?"

"Don't be naïve, Professor. We know lots of things you'll never read in your textbooks. The woman's Kar'ine. Will catch up with you the day after tomorrow. And if you actually see the PM give him *d'risot-Shalom*, best wishes, from Porcupine."

"Will he know who Porcupine is?"

"Probably not. But if he puts his mind to it he can find out. See you soon. *L'hit…*"

* * * * *

After Itamar had left the VIP apartment it was difficult for Gabby to think clearly. Of course she was disappointed by his coolness. She had expected more, but argued to herself that he was under extreme pressure. The *Yeshu* Fragment was just one more thing on his plate, one neither of them had expected.

Yet all her instincts demanded she think hard, sit down, control the nervous energy surging through her body and figure out her next move. She sat on a leather couch to cool down, but could not free her mind from the copy of the *Yeshu* Fragment hidden in the Talpiot home she shared with Itamar. She could scarcely visualize it in her mind; after having put it out of her thoughts for fourteen months it now slept in a shroud of fog. Knowing it to be a forbidden copy, she found it unpleasant to examine.

What had possessed her to break an oath and produce a copy of this sacred name was a mystery. While ruminating over the event she tried to reconstruct her previous thinking but came up empty. Too much emotion at the time. And now, too little memory left.

It occurred to her that physical exercise might relieve her tension. The gym clothes promised by the marshal were neatly hung in an armoire. She devised a plan to put on gym shorts and a tank top, and in a new pair of running shoes leave the apartment complex on foot and sprint as fast as possible to rendezvous with an Uber car. But this idea was rejected as impractical. She wouldn't get far on foot and, after all, government officials knew where she lived. Drawing attention to herself was certain to produce unwanted results.

It was the presence of a man's running jersey and training pants that triggered another solution. If she disguised herself in men's clothing it might be possible to avoid the marshal. She was certain the Prime Minister had not shared with him the reason why she was a reluctant guest of the government; there was little reason for him to suspect she might want to slip away unnoticed.

The gym clothing was several sizes too big, though synthetic fabric completely covered her feminine form. Before slipping into the corridor in her new outfit, she had the presence of mind to attach a "Do Not Disturb" notice on the door handle, hoping it would dissuade the marshal from checking in on her, at least through the afternoon and evening.

She shuffled down one flight of stairs and cautiously approached the lobby door. No sign of the marshal until she sighted him chatting with an attractive young couple, his vision of the front door partially obscured. Not enough for her to make a clean escape, yet given the fact that the passage of time had become extremely important it was a gamble worth taking. She angled her torso away from her chaperon. Hopefully, he wouldn't be expecting a male runner and allow her to jog across the street and disappear among pedestrians.

The stratagem worked. She rejected the idea of using Uber because it would provide unnecessary electronic records and elected to hail a taxi, of which there were many circulating in the government hub.

Talpiot District, Jerusalem

Itamar's home, once the residence of a Palestinian family that had fled to Transjordan during the 1948 War of Independence, was located on an early 20th Century street marked by Bauhaus architecture and shaded by scruffy plane trees. To save water, the lawn had been converted to a stone garden where Gabby had planted colorful geraniums and impatiens.

She let herself through the front door and was immediately struck by a presentiment of someone's presence. Pausing to listen in the vestibule, she heard nothing but an old-fashion European metronomic clock. In the taxi the thought that her home might have been entered by government officials crossed her mind, but she could not imagine what they might have searched for, and indeed, as she marched through the living area toward the study there were no signs of unwanted entry. Her plan was to boot up her Apple and find the *Yeshu* image on YouTube, then fetch from the Talmudic tractate her photocopy for comparison.

In the seconds required to boot YouTube, her eyes scanned the section of bookshelf dedicated to Judaica, especially the *shas*, a collection of Talmudic tractates inherited from the estate of the late Rabbi Zacharias Schreiber. As soon as the YouTube image displayed on her HD screen, she studied it to compare what she had seen in the office of the Prime Minister. It was what she remembered. Next, she conjured up a mental image of the original Yeshu Fragment from fourteen months before. It appeared to mirror what she recalled, yet she warned herself that memories are often deceptive.

And they were! To Gabby's utter horror the *Yeshu* Fragment was not in Tractate *Terumot.* She was absolutely certain that on the eventful day when she copied the parchment she had placed it carefully where it wouldn't be lost. Was it possible that Itamar had discovered and removed it? She mulled that around in her mind quickly and just as quickly dismissed the possibility. Iti had little or no interest in the rabbinic Judaism of the Talmud, the Judaism bequeathed to the Jewish people by a tight-knit hierarchy of scholar-rabbis who insisted that they were the sole arbiters of God's revelation. In contrast, he was a dedicated promoter of archeology, believing that bricks and mortar deliver the most accurate description of Jewish thought and history. That he would search her Talmudic books seemed improbable.

She felt herself frantically pulling out other tractates in the unlikely possibility that her memory had slipped. Maybe it was not *Terumot* but some other tractate. The more she scoured her memory the less she discovered. To get a fresh perspective and relieve mounting panic, she decided to leave her study and get a drink from the kitchen. But the farther she went from the place where she believed the photocopy to be, the more her mind blocked memory.

Was it possible that government officials had been there already? If they had, she reminded herself, they left no signs. And even more compelling, how would an agent have the slightest clue that a copy of the original fragment existed?

Moving back to the bookshelf, her doubts mounted. It became necessary to re-scour her memory, forcing herself to recall what her consciousness had obviously scrambled. She replayed putting the fragment upon the surface of the copy machine and remembered her hands shaking. There had been no doubt in her mind that what she was doing was in bad faith. It was a form of betrayal for which she was never proud. Yet she rationalized that so long as nobody knew a copy had been made, absolutely no damage had occurred.

She asked herself again why she had done it. Perhaps it was premonition that someday this copy could be used to verify the authenticity of the real fragment. If so, it was prescient.

She shut her eyes and reached as deep as she could into her recollections. Deeper and deeper she descended, as if the brain were a muscle that only needed stretching. Nothing came up.

Disappointment was almost palpable. Her betrayal suddenly morphed into self-anger. Clearly, she had experienced a once-in-a-lifetime opportunity to stand at the vortex of history and make a significant contribution to scholarship, but then had blown it. It was nothing short of carelessness. It was certain to haunt her, whatever the Vatican decided to do with the only physical connection to the living Jesus.

Gabby conceded that she had been beaten. Now, the better part of wisdom was to return to the VIP apartment and prepare the statement demanded by the Prime Minister. At the press conference she and Itamar would dutifully testify that in their judgment the *Yeshu* Fragment posted on YouTube was a hoax, designed to bamboozle the public.

She debated with herself a far easier question, whether or not to spend the night in her own bed or return immediately to the government apartment and wait for Itamar. Once again, the better part of wisdom required her to return immediately, rather than risk an army of police agents hunting for her.

She moved back to the study for a final survey of the library, telling herself that she should make a final attempt to find the copy. Since she was certain she had stored it inside a religious book, she decided to examine each volume of Talmud.

She began her new search by re-examining old ground and re-opened *Terumot's* threadbare binding. For the fourth time she shuffled through pages written in Aramaic in the special Rashi script. The *Yeshu* photocopy had been made on common 8x11 inch copy paper and stuffed between the tractate's soiled leaves. On this occasion Gabby chose not to begin her search in the middle and work her way toward both ends, but to start on the opening page and turn each leaf progressively forward.

Her new plan of attack produced an entirely different result.

Tucked behind the leather cover was a single sheet of white copy paper upon which was the image of the *Yeshu* Fragment!

She was so relieved that for an instant she forgot why this was so important. When she came to her senses, her eyes fell upon the name Jesus which looked like what she remembered from the Prime Minister's office. As soon as she could reboot the Internet and find the YouTube entry, a careful assessment shouldn't be difficult. She was particularly anxious to compare the color and edges that she deemed impossible to duplicate without knowing the original.

Her first task was to enlarge the digital image and then to orient her photocopy along a similar axis. In that form her eyes could move clockwise around the copy and make an accurate visual comparison. Next required a careful examination of the calligraphy, matching each of the Aramaic letters, particularly the irregular vegetable ink stains. It was inconceivable that a forger would know what irregularities to duplicate. And since only a very small coterie of individuals knew that the *Yeshu* Fragment existed, how would a forger know the fragment's dimensions?

Gabby wanted to discover compelling evidence that the document was phony. But within a minute it became obvious it wasn't. Whoever had posted the fragment's image on the Internet had access to the real thing, and this complicated Gabby's dilemma. How could she publicly deny what she knew to be true? Sooner or later it would doom her career.

Chapter Two

G abby avoided being seen by the Prime Minister's marshal who was nowhere to be seen in the lobby, suggesting he had left for a bite to eat or a bathroom break. His absence allowed her to reenter the VIP apartment. She was not surprised to learn that Itamar wasn't there. A quick calculation told her that he was likely to return in the wee hours of the morning, but certainly before noon to compose his response to the Prime Minister's demand.

Normally, she would take advantage of free time to fulfill a daily exercise routine. The basemen gym would be perfect. But she didn't feel like more than a stiff walk in which she could weigh the implications of having verified the *Yeshu* Fragment. Were there compromises to be found short of advocating a position in clear contrast with the truth? And should she reveal the photocopies existence with Itamar? The sun had long since set. Gabby found herself walking on sidewalks from which she could see the illuminated Kenesett framed against a toy-land of light from multiple high-rises condominiums scattered atop Jerusalem's hillside landscape. By the end of her peregrination through Jerusalem's government center she had a clear answer. Itamar needed to know an essential fact before facing the coming press conference.

Back in the apartment a sense of relief eased her nerves. She undressed and headed for a shower, always cognizant that in water-short Israel leisurely American showers were taboo. She soaked her body, turned off the tap to cover the skin with a delightfully smelling concierge soap, whose scent she calculated might linger if Itamar returned at a reasonable hour and showed a desire for snuggling, or more. But this she rejected as unlikely. He had been obviously distracted and despite their separation had shown little interest in her.

Since she liked to sleep without pajamas in strange hotel beds, she wrapped herself in a fluffy terrycloth bath towel. The wait for Itamar would be difficult and to pass the time she turned on a television set for distraction and found herself gazing at a screen with images dancing before her eyes. To her surprise, she became aware that she had failed to turn up the audio volume and therefore had only a partial sense of what appeared on the screen. No matter. The *Yeshu* Fragment kept reappearing in her mind's eye.

When sleep began creeping over her, she switched off the television, dropped the towel on the floor and wrestled her body under the covers of a firm and well-packed bed, still uncertain whether Itamar would return in the wee hours or make a last-minute appearance at the Prime Minister's press conference.

* * * * *

To guard against infections, Israeli physicians and medics wouldn't let Itamar enter the triage tent and he was required to wait outside. During the interval he approached Major Makket to clear Kar'ine's visa, along with a Permit of Custody placing her in his care for 14 days.

When she eventually emerged from the triage station she was on her own feet with a medical orderly holding her arm for support. This was Itamar's first sign that unlike the severely injured Syrian soldiers she was in good enough health to move on her own steam.

Her lips were sealed as he received her arm from the orderly. "I was so worried about you," he said as he leaned toward her with a welcoming kiss on the cheek.

Her eyes were moist as she regarded him, still failing to provide verbal acknowledgment. He could feel that her steps were uncertain and that she welcomed his support.

He said, "*Baruch ha-ba*," Welcome to Israel, or as we say in here, *ha-Aretz*. It's been a long time, but thank God you're finally here, safe and sound. From now on, Kar'ine, we'll take care of you. You'll find a good home here."

"Thanks, Harry," she said, using the pseudonym he used in Istanbul—Harry Kellerman from South Africa. So much has changed in my own country since the war."

"We're headed for my car and I'm going to take you to a beautiful place overlooking the Sea of Galilee where you can rest. It's a working kibbutz, but also a guesthouse, well-known for fabulous food."

"And will you remain there with me?" she inquired.

"Only for a sort time. I must dash to Jerusalem for an important meeting. But I'll return in a day or so. I have a special phone for you, and we can talk even when I'm away."

In the car moving swiftly along Highway 98, he twisted his torso to examine Kar'ine's profile with its strong Semitic nose and high cheeks. At the moment she was sitting comfortably studying the high plateau of the Golan Heights, seized from Syria during the 1967 Six Days War. "They didn't hurt you, did they?" he asked about Hezbollah agents he knew she had business with in Aleppo and Damascus.

For a long moment she said nothing before volunteering in a low voice. "No. According to Shira law, I'm technically a married woman. Though my husband is dead I have not filed the appropriate documents in a Shira court. It doesn't matter. Most of my affairs are with Lebanese businessmen and, as long as the money flows, they don't care. Arab men do business with me because they need my services. And they pay me very well. When we first met in Istanbul, Harry, I possessed only what artifacts I could bring with me from Syria. But today, *Allah Akbar*, I'm financially secure."

"Delighted, Kar'ine. You've always been talented. Good to learn they didn't harm you."

Her eyes moved from the landscape to meet with Itamar's before his returned to the road. She added, filling a momentary pause, "But they did, friend. They hurt me almost every time there was a transaction."

"How so? You look as healthy to me as ever."

"Arab men expect their women to serve them in bed. For them, an evening between the sheets is simply entertainment. Women keep them entertained."

"They forced you?" Itamar hit the brakes suddenly but from reflex released his foot and resumed the original speed.

Again a rather long silence, followed by, "No, Harry. When I arrived in Istanbul I had no friends and no supporters. You provided both, and that I will not forget. In my culture lying is very common. Trade exists because Arabs always know when they are being lied to and they accommodate for this mendacity. It's entirely cultural. But you were never part of my culture. It was refreshing to work with someone who didn't function in a world of falsehoods. I pledged then never to lie to you and I won't now. None of the Lebanese men I dealt with raped me. And none forced me against my will. A few who paid outrageous fees for my professional service expected me in their beds. I could have refused, but I didn't. I hate business like that. But it's an essential, without which I would have failed. And probably, given my husband's background and my exile in Turkey, been raped and then executed."

Itamar gulped saliva. He knew her to be a physically affectionate but far from a loose woman. What he heard was repulsive, yet he also knew her to be a shrewd businesswoman. To withhold such an intimate matter would have been easy. It was her forthrightness that had always attracted him. "Must have been horrible for you," he forced the words through his lips.

For the first time since their meeting outside the triage tent she showed a sign of feminine warmth by placing her hand on his wrist and lightly patting. "No, dear friend. Perhaps for many women it would have been a nightmare. But not for me. Until I met you, I had no relations with my husband for five years. In Damascus I compensated for that loss. I reckoned that if sex was necessary to conduct my affairs there was no useful purpose not to enjoy it. Resisting wouldn't have done anyone a good. Neither my clients, nor me. And it has certainly made my business lucrative."

What Kar'ine said was more than Itamar wanted to know, and more than he was fully prepared to accept. The notion of mixing sex with business was foreign to him, but then he reminded himself that Kar'ine had constantly surprised him. He found her not only beautiful but mysteriously exotic, totally different from other women he knew, including Gabby.

Their route south past Mount Hozek led through forested highlands then descended into manicured vineyards. Kar'ine was impressed by the cleanliness of the roadside and the abundance of private cars. Itamar became an enthusiastic guide who wanted her to be impressed by his country, the nation he anticipated would become her permanent home. He found himself chattering like a teenager about one sight after another. In the middle of this soliloquy, he noticed Kar'ine adjusting a soiled white *hijab* on the rear of her crown. "You don't have to wear that in Israel," he offered.

She returned with a smile that exposed an array of fine teeth seldom seen in Arab women. "My head has been covered since I was a child. I'm naked without it. We'll see how tolerant you Israelis really are. You say there is no prejudice here against Muslims. I'm skeptical, but we'll see, now won't we?"

The sun was setting by the time of their arrival at Kibbutz Ha-On. It seemed odd to Kar'ine that there was no formal gate and no security guards. Itamar maneuvered his Toyota to a small parking lot from which they needed to march between a series of low farm buildings to a bungalow fronting a thick pine forest. It was completely dark inside this edifice until Itamar opened a screen door and switched on an electric porch light. A second switch illuminated the single room with two beds.

"I love it," declared Kar'ine. She dropped on one of the beds and said, "You know how long I was strapped under blankets on a canvas stretcher in Syria? About 16 hours. Can you imagine being a prisoner for that long? Thank Allah, I started with not a drop in my bladder. This bed is made for a queen."

"And you are a queen, Kar'ine," he gave her strong hug and whispered into her ear, "My treasure from Istanbul."

* * * * *

It was past 3 a.m. when Itamar returned to the VIP apartment in Jerusalem. A peek into the bedroom told him that Gabby had pushed together the twin beds and was asleep under light blankets. In the bathroom he used a toothbrush provided by the management, took off his shoes and dropped his outer garments onto the floor. His steps back to the vacant bed barely produced a sound. A moment later he was under the covers listening to the air conditioning growl from wall vents.

Gabby was aware he had returned and when he was ensconced in the second bed flipped her legs from her own and stepped toward him, gently dropping down beside him. In the darkness her lips found his cheek while her hand reached under the blanket to massage his shoulder. A slight roll against him advertised that she had neither the nightgown nor the tee shirt she always wore in their Jerusalem bedroom. With no response, she pulled back his blanket and when there was sufficient room coiled her legs and forced them alongside, leaving no doubt about her readiness for lovemaking.

To her advance he half-rolled away, saying "Gabb, I'm exhausted. Sorry to have left you alone. We must talk in the morning." Disappointed, she knew that when under stress he was never interested in sex. She crawled out of his bed and re-deposited herself in her own. On her back with her head propped up by two overly fluffy pillows, she peered at the darkened ceiling above as thin tears streaked her cheeks.

It was 6:11 a.m. when she pulled out of bed, and after observing how deeply Itamar slept, stepped into the adjacent living room, carefully closing the door behind. After donning light clothing, she moved to the dining area to find it well stocked for breakfast. A Keurig coffee maker mirrored the one in her Jerusalem home. The pantry provided various breakfast cereals and the refrigerator, 2% milk. Once the coffee had brewed she marched to a panoramic window facing west into the Hills of Judea, there resuming her calculations about the *Yeshu* Fragment. Arguments about what to do marched through her brain one way and reversed to another. The pregnant fact that kept emerging was that until the posting on YouTube the fragment's secret was known only by a select few, and despite what might be known in Rome, no one in Israel including the Prime Minister knew she had made a photocopy. And if she chose to conceal that secret no one would be the wiser. Her unique knowledge would die with her.

Yet knowing the fragment to be genuine, she couldn't see herself contributing to an outright historical lie. Were this to be a mere white lie there might be some rationale. But this truth about Christianity's Savior was anything but trivial.

Itamar eventually joined her in the dining area adjacent to the efficiency kitchen, looking exhausted and in no way eager to meet the press. He had not shaved, nor for that matter made any attempt to tame his wild salt and pepper hair in need of trimming.

"There's much to talk about," Gabby lost no time setting the stage for a conversation she knew would be unpleasant. Itamar observed her retrieve a bottle of orange juice from the refrigerator, along with the container of milk. A box of cereal remained on the counter where she had left it.

"You've given thought to helping me at the press conference this afternoon, I presume," he said while filling a glass with orange juice.

"All night long, as a matter of fact," she responded. "Not an easy night, you can imagine."

"But really, there isn't a choice, is there? We have no evidence the *Yeshu* doc is real. Nobody knows that, and it's unlikely anyone will ever know one way or the other. So our part at the press conference should be easy. Nothing lost because there is no proof in the matter."

For the last time Gabby debated with herself whether to reveal what she knew. Several instincts told her to say nothing, but in the end she felt this unfair. "I have something important to report," she started with a slight stammer in her words. "Something that you must know before you go to the conference. Something absolutely critical."

"Oh…" he said, "I thought I had everything I needed."

"No, Iti, I'm afraid you don't. There's something important, you *don't* know."

He stopped fiddling with the juice glass and lifted his chin so that morning light from the window glistened over his multi-day stubble.

She had rehearsed what she would say innumerable times, tightening each version until she ran out of rehearsal time. "You remember I once called you from the Old City saying I was in possession of an historical treasure. I told you where Tim Matternly had hidden it and how I had found it after his death. You fetched me in the Old City's Zion Gate near the Church of the Ascension where I had gone to collect my thoughts. What I didn't tell you then and have never told anyone until now is that before I took the fragment with me into the Old City, I made a photocopy on Tim's Canon copy machine."

While gazing upon Gabby through wounded eyes Itamar struggled to his feet, slowly straightening his posture as though an old man climbing from a low chair. "You're telling me now, after all these months, that you made a copy! It was egregiously clear that our gag order forbade us doing that. And for fourteen months you said nothing! We shared a sacred silence, but apparently you decided to go your own way. I'm absolutely speechless!"

"I did it *before* signing the gag order…and well *before* you eventually exchanged the fragment in Rome for documents now in the Shrine of the Book."

"What deceit!" Itamar snapped with anger. "I thought we were partners. How could you have done such a horrible thing, you who everybody thinks of as the honest Rabbi Gabrielle Lewyn?"

Gabby was now also on her feet, planted on the hardwood floor as though preparing to receive a blow. "I should have told you earlier, Iti, but the fact is I didn't. Frankly, I don't know why I made the copy in the first place. For many hours last night I tried to conjure up the thoughts that went through my mind fourteen months ago. Nothing. Just a blank, although I must say in my defense, it's not unnatural to want a copy of something valuable. I knew the original belonged to the government; that's why I immediately transferred it to you as Director of Antiquities. I could have secreted it out of Israel and sold it for enough to make me a very rich woman. But I didn't. If I had, we wouldn't be together today."

Itamar expelled air through his front teeth before sealing his lips in an angry gesture. "I can't believe you'd do a thing like that to me. You were honor bound. Some fucking honor."

She snapped back. "I didn't have to tell you about this but I did. I could have kept it secret to the end of my life and nobody, absolutely nobody, would have been any the wiser."

"So why did you, lady?"

She let his hostility cool for a long instant before saying, "Because, Iti, my copy is suddenly terribly important. The YouTube image of the fragment that Sonnenberg is so exercised about is only significant if it's the true image and not, as he would want the world to think, a fake. Yesterday afternoon I went home and retrieved the copy from where I had stashed it. I swear I never once looked at it since the day I put it between the pages of Tractate *Temurot*. I almost forgot where I had put it but I needed to compare my copy of the original with the YouTube image."

Itamar's face blanched as he scrutinized Gabby's expression. She didn't finish speaking, but nodded her head positively. He turned away to gaze from the window into a cluster of condominiums faced with the pale pink Jerusalem stone on the opposite side of the apartment complex. "You've just made my job impossible. You know I have no alternative but to deny the authenticity at the press conference. You may enjoy being a free spirit around here, but I'm a paid government official and for now I want to remain one. And I can't suddenly come out and declare there's always been a fucking copy."

"I wouldn't expect that," she answered. "Now that I've compared the edges and color and the script of the YouTube image, my position isn't any easier than yours."

She stepped across the dining area to embrace him but before her open arms touched, he blocked with his forearms, striking an angry blow to Gabby's hands. "I wish you had never told me," he growled.

"How could I let you go before the press without knowing the truth? That would have been worse. Will it be easier when the world eventually learns that the fragment is genuine? Whoever posted it wanted others to know. I have no idea who that might be. Probably someone in the Vatican, but it's impossible to prove."

"Right," Itamar said, his tone raw with sarcasm. He turned to snatch a satchel had dropped in the wee hours of the morning. "I'm out of here, lady."

"Where you going?" she inquired following him through the vestibule.

"Truth is, I don't know."

"May I come with you?"

He turned to look at her while swinging his head negatively in a final gesture. A moment later he slammed the entrance door closed behind him.

* * * * *

A pervading gloom fell over Gabby; a darkness she felt might likely exclude redemption. Yes, it was still possible to show up at the press conference to perform like a circus sea lion and echo Itamar's statement about the *Yeshu* Fragment. But how could she? Did she want to end her career on an outright lie? And how was it that Itamar was incapable of understanding that she had copied the document *before* not *after* pledging a gag order? Yes of course she had copied the fragment. But ask a hundred people on the street if they would have made a photocopy of such an important document and all hundred would respond in the positive. Why couldn't Itamar understand that?

And to make matters worse, possessing this evidence threatened her safety. Two people central to the discovery of the fragment, Tim Matternly and Father Benoir Matteau, both suffered unnatural deaths.

Both, according to police reports, perished in the Judean Desert at the hands of Bedouin tribesmen who disappeared into the wilderness, leaving few traces in the sand. It had taken Gabby months to appreciate that the government regarded Father Benoir and Tim Matternly not as heroes, but as thieves, and that their Bedouin assassins had actually spared the government lengthy, embarrassing and expensive trials. Now that Benoir and Tim were dead, she, Itamar and the Prime Minister were the only witnesses to evidence confirming how Jesus trained to become a spokesman for God. And once Itamar publically denied the existence of the fragment, she would stand entirely alone, an easy target for whoever wanted to keep the fragment's existence secret.

* * * * *

Itamar had long judged Zebulon Sonnenberg to be a vindictive man, using his political power to punish those who opposed him. And in Gabby's case, failing to obey his command was certain to trigger an indictment for violation of state secrets, or worse. Sonnenberg had personally warned that he could make her life miserable.

The Prime Minister's lieutenants had assembled his heavy artillery for the press conference. Archeology was big business in Israel, supporting many families, most of whom lived in Jerusalem. When the PM commanded his leaders in the archeological trade his marionettes dutifully performed their gyrations.

Gabby had spent a terrible hour debating whether to run after Itamar and attempt reconciliation. She felt compelled to find him and explain again the sequence of events that had led to her copying the fragment. She caught up with him where she knew he must be, in the antechamber to the Knesset Press Room, circled by Rabbi Menachim Barak, David Stern, Sarah Eisenhart, Thomas Dilllingham and Shmuel Navid, all archeology scholars closely associated with his department, at the moment waiting to be ushered onto the dais to make their declarations.

When she tugged at his arm from behind he twisted about to lock his vision on her, before saying, "I'm glad you've changed your mind, Gabb."

She pulled him farther from the circle of professionals and waited until assured no one might overhear. "I haven't," she declared. "I've tried to understand what is being achieved here and cannot see my way

32

clear to add my voice. I came only because I knew this is where I'd find you. Because I wanted to explain the sequence of events leading to my copy of the fragment."

Itamar inhaled and for a second held his breath. "Don't bother. But if you're determine to run with this matter on your own, you need to be reminded that your best chance of staying alive is let the Prime Minister put you into protective custody. Don't forget, you had to bury Tim Matternly, and I had to make ludicrous excuses to the Vatican when Benoir Matteau was slaughtered in the desert."

"I'm not unaware of this," she responded. "Don't think for a moment this is my first choice."

"Sonnenberg won't let you run around this country free. If I read him correctly, he'll fulfill his threats against you."

A press officer announced aloud that the moment had arrived for the participants to file through a side door leading into the conference room. It was necessary for him to repeat instructions in a louder voice to command attention. Within seconds the pack went into motion.

A look of despair clouded Itamar's face as he glance about to determine how much time he had left. "Are you with us, Gabb?" he almost pleaded. "Are you coming with me?" he repeated, emphasizing the word *me*.

She allowed herself to be swept forward for several steps, but then stopped abruptly. "No, Iti. I cannot."

The conference officer herded the scholars through the door and held it open while he motioned with his arm for Gabby to hurry up. In a final moment of indecision she took still another step forward, knowing that time had run its course. This was her final chance. But the same logic, the same flow of events, the same compelling notion that she was standing at the vortex of history compelled her to halt, and with an open palm signaled for the door to be shut. An instant later she found herself alone in an empty antechamber, more alone than she had ever felt in her life.

* * * * *

Itamar's performance at the press conference left much to be desired. As moderator he was expected to control conversation about the *Yeshu* Fragment by directing his team of experts to respond accordingly to questions pitched by an alert and aggressive press corp. That would have demanded all his attention, but the reality was different. His breakup with Gabby produced an empty feeling in his gut along with unwanted moisture in his eyes that an acute observer might have identified as tears. His nervousness was apparent; not what the Prime Minister wanted from his antiquities director, especially when pitching a dubious hypothesis about the YouTube entry.

Even more than sadness over losing Gabby were his trepidations about her safety. It was bad enough to know a forbidden detail of Christian history and to become involved in the murky deaths of Tim Matternly and Father Benoir, without having now incurring the enmity of the Israeli Prime Minister. Fortunately, as Itamar cascaded into his dark thoughts, Rabbi Menachim Barak on the dais seized time before the cameras to explain a personal view of Jewish life in First Century Palestine while conveniently referring to a scholarly book he had authored on a tangential subject.

About the dangerous road ahead for Gabby, Itamar felt compelled to do something. In the oppressive pressure of the press conference he could devise nothing more than a simple warning. While Rabbi Barak expanded his exegesis, Itamar punched out on his I-Phone a text message addressed to Gabby's cell number and immediately dispatched it into cyberspace.

Best to attend cousin's funeral in New York

Chapter Three

Papal Secretary of State Donaldo Cardinal Fornetti eased back in his conference chair to settle his vision upon Monsignor Guido Capalliani, Director of the Vatican Archive before allowing it to drift sideways upon the Reverend Monsignor Erwin Nebdal, Director for the Teutonic College of Sacred Archeology. At the opposite end of the conference table an oversized television screen displayed a panel of Israeli antiquities authorities ending a press conference in Jerusalem. For a long moment none of the Vatican officials offered interpretations for the extraordinary event they had just witnessed streamed from Israeli television.

Donaldo Cardinal, who had risen through Curia bureaucracy with precipitous starts and stops (even a brief and what his peers believed to be an unsubstantiated accusation of pedophilia), expressed alarm over viewing the YouTube image of the *Yeshu* Fragment. He had been the Pope's personal negotiator with the Government of Israel over this unique parchment and had assured the Holy Father that its existence would remain a secret until the Church was ready to provide a theological response. That response was still being formulated and, given the Church's long-term perspective, might take many more years. But then suddenly out-of-the-blue, the appearance of this fragment on YouTube changed everything! Taken out of context this leak was bound to spawn popular misunderstanding—just what the Holy Father didn't want!

In addition to his other duties, Donaldo looked upon himself as protector of the Catholic Church, charged by the Curia to respond to emergencies such as this. Having been one of two negotiators to acquire this priceless fragment from the Government of Israel in exchange for the less valuable fragments secreted from Qumran to Rome by Father Benoir Matteau fourteen months before, he believed the Church had been betrayed, but by whom he was uncertain. The Vatican and Jerusalem had signed an unconditional gag order on all matters concerning this fragment. And then, suddenly the name of Jesus had gone viral on YouTube! In Rome, that's all people were talking about. Chatter from the devout all over the world was particularly disturbing.

That the Government of Israel had reacted immediately to deny the fragment's existence Donaldo regarded as a good sign. He had little doubt that under his direction the Church of Rome would respond in kind, firmly denying such a fragment ever existed. If only that would be the end of it. But his instincts told him that this unfortunate affair was just beginning.

"I suspect we're all relieved to see that the Government of Israel is officially as worried as we," Donaldo finally said, having settled his gaze upon Monsignor Nebdal, "Erwin, I know you and Guido have had little time for a thorough investigation, but I want to know who you think is responsible for this mess."

A throaty grumble seemed to get stuck in Guido Capallini's throat as though he was reluctant to speak until after Nebdal voiced his opinion. In the momentary hiatus he said, "You're right, Donaldo. Not much time at all, but then the field is narrow. Only a few have been privileged to know of this treasure. Monsignor Nebdal and I have looked at all the potential culprits. In Jerusalem there's only the late Prime Minister Rahav, and the now current PM Sonnenberg along with Doctor Arad, Director for Israel Antiquities, a man with whom I had close dealings during the exchange. I doubt seriously that he was the leaker, even if he had a motive, which I don't believe he has. Itamar Arad is a thorough professional and, as far as we can determine, a loyal servant of the Jewish state. And that leaves only one suspect—Rabbi Gabrielle Lewyn, who it is said to have found the fragment among papers of the late Timothy Matternly. These days she works at the Shrine of the Book. Our people who have read her scholarly contributions believe she is no friend of the Church. Our assessment is that she is what some would call a "free spirit," undisciplined and quite willing if not eager to engage the Holy See in theological argument."

"You believe that Rabbi Lewyn is the leaker then?" asked Donaldo.

"We eliminated all potential culprits; she's the only one left standing, and one who while a respected scholar is certainly not an admirer of the Church."

Donaldo Cardinal nervously massaged loose skin beneath his jaw before drawing the skin flaps tight from his cheeks. "Well let's acknowledge, gentlemen, our dilemma. The fragment is now in the public domain, and I'm afraid we can do nothing to rescue it from universal knowledge. We all know its existence should not remain secret forever. But now is not the right time to disclose it; and most certainly not via YouTube."

"Serious dilemma, yes?" commented Guido Capalliani in an acknowledging uplift of his voice."

"Without question…and more serious than we might imagine."

"Is there something we should be doing?" pursued Capalliani.

Donaldo's lips tightened, rounding a well-manicured moustache whose light gray hue made it almost undistinguishable from the upper lip. He said, "In my judgment the publication of the fragment is little danger in and of itself. The fact that we now have concrete evidence that our Lord lived when and where we have always believed will only fortify our faith. No, the fragment in itself is little threat to our belief." The cardinal paused to evaluate how his colleagues received this view. And when he failed to find a sign that they disagreed continued, "The danger is where this fragment was discovered. It does us no good that the purported name of our Lord was found on a list of students at a Judean school allegedly founded to prepare prophets for their sacred task. Our enemies will use that to argue that Lord Jesus was no more than a prophetic do-gooder, to undermine the Preacher's divine nature. And when the Trinity is weakened so will the authority of the Church."

"Rabbi Lewyn? What about her?" Nebdal interrupted the cardinal's oration.

"She's the danger. I hoped you took notice that she was not present at the Jerusalem press conference. In fact, two speakers drew attention to her absence. Remember seeing an empty seat for her at the dais? It looked as if the Jewish officials expected to hear her views and were perturbed she was not there. Why? For that question I have no answer, other than she did not wish to deny that the fragment existed. She obviously refused to take a public stance."

"Do we know her next move?"

"No. But we know she's involved in making a film about the late Timothy Matternly who discovered the fragment in Cave XII. As we speak, a production crew is preparing for this in the desert near Sodom. That's near where this school for prophets is thought to have operated. Lewyn will no doubt include this in her documentary about Professor Matternly. Our people in Jerusalem should be able to track her down."

"And then what?" queried Father Nebdal.

"Then…" and here the cardinal hesitated before lowering his voice as if to keep his words more secret than they already were, "If it's not too late, Rabbi Lewyn must be prevented from disclosing details about the fragment. And here, my friends, we might have to act independently from the Jewish government in Jerusalem."

"Are we too late?"

"At this moment we have no knowledge she has revealed anything more than the fragment itself. But she's a time bomb that could explode any minute. It is our responsibility to see she does not explode."

Nebdal grunted vocally and followed by rolling his top lip over his teeth. It appeared he wanted to speak but once again respectfully conceded to his colleague. Guido Capalliani filled in the silence. "Must we read through the lines, Donaldo? Is what you're hinting what the Holy Father wants?"

The cardinal snapped back with a sharp response. "The Holy Father is above such worldly matters and must remain so. This is the kind of work He delegates to his servants such as you and me."

"Will you raise the matter before Him?"

"I most certainly will not. His Holiness is the Vicar of Life and must remain above worldly matters, especially when they touch the dark side of reality. Rabbi Lewyn has betrayed our trust. We returned Professor Matternly's treasures to Israel in good faith in exchange for a solemn pledge, which this woman has violated. She has brought this darkness upon herself. You, Gentlemen, may remain aloof. Leave the matter in my hands. I demand that you give me your silence. And once done, no more will be spoken about it. Let it just slip away into time. I act with the complete conviction that this is in the best interest of the Eternal Church."

Chapter Four

Best to attend cousin's funeral in New York

At first Gabby was thoroughly perplexed by Itamar's text message. He knew she had no cousins in New York. And what was more confusing, none of her cousins in Los Angeles and San Francisco had died! Itamar was well aware her family was intact.

Under normal conditions one would simply ask for clarity but Itamar obviously didn't want direct communication and provided a single sentence to convey his thinking. His odd message forced her to read between the lines. The phony funeral was a pretext. He must have been advising her to flee from Zebulon Sonnenberg's long arm. And since Jewish funerals customarily occurred within a day or so after death, he was also urging her to leave the country immediately.

None of that really made much sense. Running from Israeli law, especially when she profoundly believed she had done nothing wrong, was not her style. Moreover, it seemed reasonable that the Prime Minister would think twice before carrying out his pledge of punishment and risk having the matter of the *Yeshu* Fragment explode into a public relations disaster. She considered flight to the States. The idea merited consideration, promising her time to evaluate the chances of rebuilding her relationship with Itamar. All her rabbinic experience had taught her how time possesses a healing component. But even more importantly, it was reasonable to believe that the YouTube leaker would return to cyberspace. And that would release her once and for all from the shackling gag-rule. In time the scandal was bound to dissipate. Time, in this context, was her ally; but in the short run she'd either have to abandon her life in Israel or find a place of temporary refuge.

* * * * *

Gabby and Lydia Browner went back a long time. The sister of her first secretary at Congregation Ohav Shalom in Washington DC, Lydia was, and remained in Gabby's opinion, the most beautiful female she had ever come to know. And that included Farryda Sorel, whom Gabby believed took honors on the scale of feminine beauty. How different they were: Lydia was a light-complexioned, dusty-haired Hellenic beauty, while Farryda a dark-skinned, jet black-haired Semite goddess. Either one could motivate armies of infatuated suitors with a faint smile of recognition. But, given the oddities of feminine hormones, neither Lydia nor Farryda showed much interest in men.

In Gabby's earlier days, Lydia Browner had been her tennis coach, teaching her to play an aggressive game during a period in her life when it was difficult to accept the notion of trouncing an opponent by using any and all methods in her arsenal including dirty shots. On the tennis court Lydia was an unapologetic bully, an assertive ball-busting female champion who refused to accept anything short of complete victory, and that involved fierce combat with men. Her physical perfection, sculpted and molded by extensive exercise and a highly-disciplined low-fat diet, always attracted a male audience at the courts. It was never clear to Gabby whether it was her beauty or tennis skill that charmed them. Most likely both.

In the early days of their friendship Lydia was bi-sexual and unabashedly promiscuous. There were short intervals when she concentrated on male bedfellows, but in the course of time her preference shifted toward the ladies. Much to her lovers' consternation, she tired of them far faster than they tired of her, leaving behind a sullied wake of broken hearts, but only long enough to be converted into lifelong friends.

Gabby's willingness to accept Lydia's love life produced its own misunderstanding. It led Lydia to believe that she might be a future bedfellow and her reluctance to crawl between the sheets with this beauty was only a matter of time. Though the goddess of love was not accustomed to being rejected she recognized Gabby was different from the others and accordingly resolved to be patient.

In Washington, Lydia and Gabby had played doubles tennis together until separated by their careers. Communication was limited to Skype and email. It became clear to Gabby early that however proficient Lydia was in tennis, the sport was not large enough to contain her. That prescience proved true when she moved into TV sport commentary where her screen presence and sports expertise commanded six-figure salaries. She eventually moved from Washington to New York and with a coterie of equally ambitious women founded Warpath Enterprises, a media production company dedicated to servicing professional sport teams. Still, there was a limit to how much work this highly temperamental, in-your-face lesbian team might get in a predominately men's world. Warpath Enterprises remained solvent only because Lydia's seven-member team lived communally in apartments without families to support.

When the publication of Tim Matternly's discoveries made Gabby into an international celebrity, Lydia proposed to feature her in a series of documentaries about the life and deeds of successful women. Gabby's pioneering work on early Christian thought promised a wide Christian audience. A film featuring her was not high on her agenda, but it was just what the Shrine of the Book needed to stimulate donations from abroad.

The idea of filming at Qumran and the wilderness school of Ein Aurum caught Lydia's fancy. Gabby began writing the script, but it proved to be more taxing than she originally believed, largely because Lydia was unexpectedly controlling and didn't share her scholarly approach. Differences in style and execution almost doomed the project in its early stages. To be near Ein Aurum for filming this desert documentary, Lydia moved four of her companions from New York to the Israeli village of Sodom, a hot, dusty desert community that clung to cliffs above the Dead Sea. As it turned out, Lydia had problems more pressing than the script.

Warpath Productions was design to function much like an Israeli kibbutz with work shared equally by all the members. Lydia's *girls*, as she liked to call them, enjoyed an unabashed openness regarding sex, where partner switching was not uncommon. At the beginning Lydia believed this reflected their free, artistic spirits. But as time evolved, she regarded the policy as a mistake. Girls who were exceedingly cooperative and willing to work long hours even in the hot isolation of

Sodom became jealous, scrappy alley cats once in bed. Dina Yelowitz and Kaitlin Morgan actually came to fisticuffs, resulting in a senseless, superficial stabbing that sent Dina to the Sodom Medical Clinic for six stitches. Her association with Warpath ended when she abandoned the troop and returned to New York. Kaitlin Morgan followed a week later, reducing the team by half.

Gabby's unexpected telephone call from Jerusalem asking to stay with the company in Sodom for a least a week perplexed Lydia. Her initial reaction was negative, thinking Gabby far too straight-laced for her hyper-sensitive girls. Yet upon further reflection, she changed her mind. If nothing else, her friend was good at calming strained emotions.

"Accommodations are cramped," she told Gabby during the phone call. "I had a devil of a time finding space in this mosquito heaven. With so little to choose from, rent here is atrocious. Finally made a deal for a decrepit, poorly air-conditioned hostel, if you can call it that, with a dozen negative stars on TripAdvisor. If you're set on coming, you'll have to bunk with my team. They'll probably be delighted to have a fresh body to mall, but if that's okay, you're welcome. And don't expect me to bail you out. You'll have to fight your own alley cat scraps. I've got enough trouble without adding another."

Gabby did not share with Lydia why it was necessary to leave Jerusalem. She would have preferred private accommodations, but then she was in no condition to be picky.

* * * * *

After collecting Kar'ine from Kibbutz Ha-On, Porcupine drove her through the Judean Valley to the ancient town of Jericho where her archeological curiosity was stirred. Upon this enthusiastic student of ancient peoples the centrality of Jericho's antiquity and geography were not lost. Porcupine was disinclined to become her private guide to Israel. Such function he wisely reserved for Itamar; still he understood the importance of pleasing this erudite woman, who through her dealings in Syria had become a source of information about the Shia fighters of Hezbollah, Israel's perennial Lebanese enemy. The unexpected had occurred when Hezbollah, strapped for money, morphed into a mercenary army, selling its military services to the faltering Syrian government in Damascus. And while this well-organized and highly disciplined group of fighters shifted its power alongside Israel's Syrian frontier, it significantly reduced a military threat on her northern border with Lebanon.

It was Itamar who first brought Kar'ine to Mossad's attention. She had been a valuable aide pursuing the illegal trade of Palestinian artifacts in Istanbul. Who better for Mossad's purposes than a modern Muslim woman from Aleppo who spoke fluent Syrian Arabic and who through her late husband was well connected in the art and antiquities worlds? No one in Mossad's rather thin arsenal of operatives in Syria was better qualified to monitor Hezbollah's movements. And yet, in Porcupine's mind, while Kar'ine appeared to be an ideal agent, she was far from perfect. For a start she wasn't Jewish, and that presented a question of loyalty. And, prior to her current visit, she had never set foot in the Jewish state. So to Porcupine her contributions would always remain suspect. Moreover, good observer of people that he felt himself to be, he sensed that her relationship with Itamar was more than professional. Experience had taught him how romance complicated intelligence gathering.

Cautioning himself that none of Mossad's agents operating in Arab nations were perfect and that each provided an element of risk, he was prepared to forgive Kar'ine for making far more money from her antiquities trade in a few months than he would earn during his career as a government employee.

Instead of heading immediately into the Hills of Judah and their Jerusalem destination, he steered his badly-in-need-of-a-wash Subaru to the site of ancient Jericho where Kar'ine prevailed upon him to stroll through the archeological park's legendary ruins. Out of caution he insisted she disguise herself in a jet-black *abaya* and wear dark glasses. It was unlikely anyone in Occupied Palestine would recognize her, but then he was always conscious that just as his associates operated in foreign lands, so Israel's enemies operated in the Jewish state.

He explained to Kar'ine that the better part of Israel's population was crazy about archeology. It seemed that every Israeli family had its resident expert. And many of these enthusiasts possessed collections of illegal antiquities. So universal was this practice that Itamar's Department of Antiquities could do little to enforce the law. Few citizens supported a program whereby the Israel Government confiscated illegal property. Itamar kept his job because he was an astute politician, able to maintain his balance on a slippery slope between public and private interests.

Once inside the Jericho park, Porcupine confessed to Kar'ine that archeology was far from his personal passion. Yet for her sake, he was not dismissive of a hobby he personally believed to be rather silly. She, on the other hand, took little notice of him, immediately immersing herself in ruins of an ancient Canaanite settlement made famous by the biblical records of Joshua's conquest. Her own academic expertise focused on Syria-Mesopotamia, not Palestine. Still, students of the ancient world understood how little modern political borders meant in the past. She would have wanted to take photographs but Porcupine had insisted that she leave behind Itamar's camera-phone. For reasons she had yet to discern the Mossad agent seemed determined to deal with her separately from Itamar. One would have thought that two policeman would work in tandem. When the question arose, Porcupine maintained that, in fact, Itamar was entirely in the picture, a situation she doubted.

After an extended detour in Jericho, Porcupine drove to Jerusalem's King David Hotel in time for lunch on the veranda overlooking the Roman and Turkish walls surrounding the Old City. Kar'ine's *abaya* was even more important in Jerusalem than in Jericho. The King David had long been an international crossroad for government and commercial officials. Though still unlikely she might be recognized, Porcupine insisted she maintain a low profile. He refused two tables offered by the maître d'hotel and ultimately settled on one in the shadows where from his years in the spy business he practiced sitting with his back to a stone wall.

The menu was continental, but after a few inquiries addressed to a Palestinian waiter Porcupine ordered an assortment of Oriental salads he felt would appeal to his Syrian guest. Her dark, almost blue eyes drew him into an embarrassing stare. He noticed how they moved, absorbing the motion of the table staff serving others. He wanted them to settle upon him, but they refused. He had witnessed this constant wariness in other agents.

To focus her attention he said, "If you haven't already noticed, my country is obsessed with security. Itamar must have shared with you a bit of our history. It shouldn't be a secret to an educated woman that we live in a hostile neighborhood, making us suspicious of just about everybody."

She sighed briefly before fashioning an omniscient smile that filled in her high cheekbones. "So I've noticed. My clothes are obvious. Everyone here can see I'm an Arab woman. Possibly one of your enemies. In my country I doubt a Jew in frock coat and heavy hat would receive equal treatment."

A jerk of his head acknowledged his agreement. "In Israel we live in a dream world. We dream of finding respectful neighbors like you, Arabs who don't hate us for our history. Our dream is to find sophisticated Arabs who can understand why we insist upon living in this special sliver of the Middle East. But while we dream we must also defend ourselves."

Iced-fruit juice arrived, along with a basket of lunch breads, no pita. Porcupine took the pause to press a new line of thinking. "Tomorrow we're going to meet with representatives of an American-European museum consortium. Not directly because they're in New York and Berlin. We'll talk by secured Skype. This meeting will be strange because the representatives hardly know of you, and I'm sure you don't want them to know your identity. Also, nobody's really sure about the legality of purchasing antiquities under the table. Procuring artifacts in wartime from Syria presents legal issues that we haven't got time to sort out. Now having said that, I want to address a matter that must have arisen in your mind. That's Itamar's role in this."

Porcupine placed his fork on a salad plate to signal the importance of what he was about to disclose. Kar'ine immediately sensed this and imitated him by settling her knife on her own plate.

"You know that Itamar is a policeman, tasked with preserving Israel's past. And in this role he must be above all suspicion. Honest and transparent in everything. Were his position to be diminished by scandal, the fabric of our nation's reverence for its past might disintegrate. We cannot allow him to be implicated in a tawdry business of secreting artifacts from Syria. No matter how lofty our ideals about preserving history, secret trading in Syrian artifacts is still a dirty business. Itamar doesn't need to know about your association with Hezbollah. And if he's smart, which we all concur he is, he won't ask. We'd like to keep him out of the rescue of Syria's artifacts." After an instant's pause, Porcupine extended the lower row of teeth beyond the uppers and wheezed, "At least for the present. And by the way, I'm told the Americans are quite pleased with the stuff you've already brokered for them. I think they look upon your previous work as a trial. And we can assume that since they are now willing to discuss the acquisition of more artifacts, you've passed the initial test. Equally important from our perspective, they haven't raised complaints about the cost. Were I the paymaster for these transactions, I'd be screaming, but fortunately that's not my business. My guess is that Americans will cough up the funds needed. They're the only people crazier about archeology than Israelis. But that's only half our bargain. If you're serious about living in this country, you're going to have to be more forthcoming about Hezbollah. The tidbits you've fed us so far aren't useful. Too general. We need to know exactly who you're dealing with."

Kar'ine's head swayed from one side to another and stopped only when the waiter who had produced a second round of salads left the table. Porcupine began to serve but suddenly stopped and signaled for her to help. While receiving Porcupine's empty plate, she resounded, "My associates trust me. Break that trust and I couldn't do you or your country any good, much less the wealthy museum donors in America and Europe."

Porcupine raised his fork to move a mound of spiced eggplant onto a piece of bread, saying, "We understand your predicament. We know how Arabs do business. Still, my bosses complain that in your antiquities trade we're the poor cousins. Americans and Europeans are getting Syrian treasures. So they're delighted to be preserving the past. And you? Well, I don't know your commission arrangements. My guess is that you buy treasures at far less than you actually trade, which means you've become a wealthy woman. In this case, everybody's happy but, of course, the poor cousins. Keep in mind that it's my organization that maintains the Americans in the game."

"If I stay alive," Kar'ine curled her lips in an acknowledging expression. Still, the part about poor cousins did not go unnoticed.

"When can I call Itamar?" she asked. She didn't wait for an answer before posing a second question she meant to ask as soon as practicable. "Can you tell me about Gabrielle Lewyn?"

This inquiry confirmed Porcupine's suspicion that there was more to her relationship with Itamar than an Israeli visa. Since Kar'ine would learn about Gabrielle Lewyn soon enough, there was no purpose in withholding what facts he knew. "Rabbi Lewyn's an American who is something of a mystery in Israel," he said, curling his lips to accompany a slight wag of his head. "In my country, we don't have female rabbis. Our women, like those in your country, stay at home and have babies and don't become professionals. And we don't understand her thinking about Judaism. Our rabbis follow an ancient code that cements our present to our past. Without this anchor we'd be just another feuding tribe in the Middle East. Gabrielle Lewyn is too much of a free-thinker for our tastes."

"Oh," Kar'ine released a huff of air. She had inferred as much.

Porcupine continued, "I hear through the rumor mill that she has connections with the Prime Minister, but that's not something I can confirm. She's become the go-to expert on the work of her deceased boyfriend, Reverend Timothy Matternly, who's responsible for discovery and decipherment of Dead Sea documents from Cave XII. She holds a position at the Shrine of the Book where Matternly's discoveries are now exhibited. You'll be fascinated to see them, along with the original Dead Sea documents. By the way, how's your Aramaic? I understand there are a few communities in northern Syria which still speak the ancient language."

"Such people are not my kin," she replied with a sudden huff. To bring the conversation back to Gabby, she said, "I've long known that Itamar would only get involved with a woman as distinguished as Gabrielle. And from a brief meeting with her in the Istanbul bazaar, I remember how attractive she is." Kar'ine released a nervous chuckle. "When I met her in Istanbul she introduced herself as an antiquities buyer from Chicago, not a rabbi and certainly not as Itamar's partner. It was clear she knew nothing about Turkish or Syrian antiquities. So why was she in Istanbul?"

"Perhaps looking for Itamar."

Again Kar'ine produced a smile of approval. "I came to the same conclusion. She's obviously in love with him. Oh, don't you worry. If your people grant me a visa I have no intention of interfering. I don't belong here. You know this and so does everybody else. I'll survive in this country but only as a guest."

"I can't understand why a woman like you wants to live in Israel."

"Have I an alternative? The home of my deceased husband in Syria lies in ruins. Today, no non-observant woman like me has a secure place in the Muslim world."

This was not a discussion Porcupine wanted to have and chided himself for bringing up the subject. The remainder of their conversation focused upon her observations of clientele lunching on the veranda of the King David.

Porcupine waited at the hotel's reception desk until a multilingual attendant provided Kar'ine with an electronic key to a room on the fifth floor, facing east overlooking Jerusalem's ancient walls. In a departing moment he whispered, "I don't suspect anyone here will recognize you. But be careful. Order your meals in your room. And though I know you'd like to get out and walk around, please don't. There will be time for this later. And by the way, you're the guest of the Israel government. No checks and no credit cards. The smaller footprint you leave the better, if you understand me."

She nodded affirmatively.

* * * * *

On the drive east to the Golan Heights Itamar's mind was distracted. The turn of events with Gabby had unnerved him. To think that a generous and loving relationship might have come to an unpredictable end was saddening. He tried but just couldn't banish from his mind the fact that in making a copy of the fragment Gabby had betrayed his trust. Sure, he understood her point about when she made the copy. But not to tell him still amounted to a painful violation of personal intimacy that they had once shared. He asked himself time and again how could this happen. And each time he arrived at the same bewilderment. Once his faith in her had been shattered there seemed to be little hope for reconciliation. Of equal worry was her security. Having been a policeman to the most vicious and unseemly part of the antiquities business no one knew better than he how scarce artifacts fostered violence. Unguarded and somewhat naïve, Gabby presented an easy target. To eliminate her would be no more difficult or unseemly than the executions of Professor Timothy Matternly or Father Benoir Matteau. Yes, he could warn her, but how might he protect her without drawing the attention of the Prime Minister, whom he calculated had an interest in her silence. He didn't believe Sonnenberg would actually injure her, but at the same time would probably not interfere with others who might.

As his Toyota approached the kibbutz he wrestled with a premonition that things were not right. Though two weeks late, Kar'ine's transfer from Syria had gone almost without a hitch. It was almost too easy. Usually, something happened at the last minute to thwart sensitive exchanges such as this. And while the IDF succeeded in exchanging many wounded fighters it had never accepted a civilian, especially someone in the employ of the Jewish state.

Traffic was abominable. Israel's population was exploding, not only in the major metropolises but in expanding suburbs. And each new family in the Occupied Territory of Palestine needed a car. On overcrowded highways Waze software could provide few alternative routes. As the Toyota climbed into the hills south of the Sea of Galilee traffic thinned and he made better progress.

Once at Kibbutz Ha-On, Kar'ine was not in the cabin where he had left her. The sun had already set beyond the Sea of Galilee, blanketing the kibbutz in impenetrable darkness. Perplexed by her absence, he considered where she might be. It was far too dark for strolling along one of the many kibbutz walking paths. A few stragglers from dinner remained in *cheder-ochal,* the dining room, sipping tea. Kar'ine was not among them. Next, it occurred to him to call the secured phone he had left with her. But damned! Kar'ine had left it on the bed stand. A brief inspection told him it had not been used since he had given it to her.

A call to Porcupine went unanswered so he left a voice-mail message. He debated whether to return to Jerusalem or call in a favor from associates in the Shin Bet. Returning to his home in Talpiot was even more problematic. It was certain Gabby wouldn't be there and the thought of an empty house was painful. Better, he reasoned, to stay in the cabin at Ha-On and wait to hear from Porcupine.

The *ceder ochal* provided after dinner coffee and fruit juices, along with a platter of left over breakfast and lunch snacks. Itamar returned to the cabin and was relieved to discover Kar'ine's toilet articles and a scarf provided by the IDF when she crossed from Syria. He acknowledged to himself that events of the past two days had exhausted him. After taking off his shoes he stretched out on top of the bedspread and immediately fell asleep.

His cell phone rang at an hour past midnight, startling him awake. The phone was secured which told him the caller was important.

"Iti, that you?" an unfamiliar voice scrambled by encoded cipher greeted him.

Still drowsy, he responded, "*Cain*, yes. *Mi atah*, who are you?"

"Porcupine. Sounds like you're asleep. Sorry to awaken you, but you called me."

Itamar gathered his wits quickly and said, "I did. Kar'ine Salik is gone. When I return to Ha-On she wasn't there. Haven't heard a word."

"Not to worry, friend. She's fine. In our keeping as a matter-of-fact. Now resting for meetings tomorrow."

"What the hell do you mean, 'In our keeping?'" Itamar growled his hostility.

"We picked her up this afternoon."

"She's not the business of Mossad. She belongs to me and the Department of Antiquities. The favor she did for you in Syria is over now. Kar'ine's free to make a new life for herself *ba-Aretz,* in Israel. That was our deal in Istanbul. She's paid her bill to this country many times over. She's safe and she's here, and that's the way it must be. If you play hardball I'll go to the Prime Minister. He owes me big time for many things, and I swear to you I won't let Mossad use Kar'ine again."

An artificial laugh echoed in Itamar's phone. When Porcupine controlled his laughter he said, "Don't go there, Iti. You know that neither the Prime Minister nor the Cabinet gets involved in Mossad business. And you also know why. We're not political. The service we provide is for the nation, not a political party. The Government won't touch this because it doesn't want to know exactly what we do and especially how we do it."

Itamar had to admit to himself that there was truth in what Porcupine had said. "Where's she now?"

"We'll have her back at Ha-On in three days. Don't worry, she's in good hands."

"How come I don't believe that? And if you're thinking of sending her back to Syria, the answer is no. No. Absolutely not! She's already done her service. And she doesn't need to prove herself further."

For a long moment there was a silent hiatus in the conversation, until Porcupine finally returned, "We'll talk about that, friend, when Kar'ine is returned to the Golan."

"Why this secrecy?" Itamar barked.

"Just remember, she's not your property or the property of the Department of Antiquities. Kar'ine's become quite important to us. She knows a lot we need to know."

"I expect her in good health," Itamar interrupted. "And I'm warning you now, Aaron, Eli, David, Naphtali or whatever's your fucking real name is, I'm going to fight for her. I won't let you fuck up her life for some lofty service to the Jewish state. She's not Israeli and, let me remind you, she's isn't Jewish. Keep you mitts off her. She's mine, Asshole…"

Porcupine snapped back with irritation. "Dr. Arad. Please remember we're on the same side here. She'll be well taken care of. Hard not to take her seriously. Urbane and witty. And what's obvious, she's not bad on the eyes either. If the Arab world had more erudite women like her we wouldn't be in our perennial pickle barrel."

"And you'd be out of a job."

A grunt traveled through cipher as a squeak. "Perhaps so, Doctor. Be patient. We'll have Salik back to you shortly. No worse for wear."

"Remember, she's not headed back into Syria. Over my dead body."

The phone clicked silent. Connection severed.

* * * * *

The following morning, clothed in her *abaya*, Kar'ine entered the main entrance of the Israel Museum. Porcupine would have directed her with his hand on her arm, but this he knew to be a violation of Arab custom so he urged her in a subdued voice not to become distracted by the exhibitions organized along a time-line of Israel's ancient past. "I know you'd love to linger here, but we can't stay. We're headed upstairs to a video room with a connection to New York and Berlin. Our meeting starts," and here he glanced down at an aviation style watch, "in exactly six minutes. Can't be late."

Kar'ine objected being herded yet she was also aware of Porcupine's motive. She prided herself on flexibility and there were multiple reasons to be cooperative. By her reckoning, one more trip to Damascus, one last excursion to this terrible place, would provide her with sufficient funds to sustain herself for the better part of a lifetime. Her secret for survival was to control her needs. Being a refugee had sucked from her all pretentions. A stranger in Israel, a stranger in her native country of Syria, a stranger in Turkey, she steeled herself with self-sufficiency. To be financially independent she must keep her wits, the very wits no one expected to find in a Muslim woman.

The video-conference room was on the museum's fourth floor, empty except for a video operator who sat Kar'ine at the head of a table and directed a camera to display her image on a 65-inch screen. The technician told her to expect the images of others displayed on a large monitor directly ahead. She could talk freely to those on the screen and not to worry about the sound. Technicians would scramble voices in New York. Porcupine took a seat off to the left in the shadows.

At the prescribed time, the New York screen flickered, then revealed the logo of the J Paul Getty Museum in Los Angeles, followed by the logo for the Deutsches Historisches Museum on Unter der Linden in the German capital.

Kar'ine was not surprised that the images of the responders were purposely blurred to conceal their identities. Each was introduced by a controller with an assumed name, all Kar'ine assumed to be financial counselors to major museums: The Getty in Los Angeles, the Metropolitan in New York, the National Museum in Washington DC, the British Museum in London, and the Deutsches Historisches in Berlin.

Kar'ine bid them good morning in English and each in turn issued a greeting. The Washington representative introduced herself stating that she would monitor the discussion. "Just call me *America* and we shall refer to you as *Syria*, if you're not offended," announced the representative from Washington.

"That works for me," responded Kar'ine.

"We're aware of how delicate this rescue is," continued *America*. "We're also aware we're a bit late in this enterprise. Much of the treasures we hope to recover are already gone. Still, our friends in Israel, who know more about the Middle East than we do, think you're still our best chance to rescue what's left. Israel tells us that you're asking for an open check to buy these artifacts. Is that true, Syria?"

Kar'ine had already decided to be completely forthright about money. "Yes, that's exactly what I'm asking."

"Why can't we provide funds as needed, or as required in your negotiations?" the German delegate pursued.

A pre-rehearsed response came to Kar'ine's lips. "Under normal business negotiations this would be reasonable. But not in Syria and not during civil war. There's no orderly auctioning as in your countries. First, I'm not dealing with professional dealers on the other side of the table. Some are educated middlemen; others little better than street thugs. Second, I'm dealing with different individuals all the time. They're government and non-government opportunists who for a short time happen to control artifacts they hope will generate immediate cash."

"But with modern communications consulting with us shouldn't be difficult," said Germany.

"Not true. How long do you think I'd last if caught? My contacts know my money comes from the West, but they can't admit that publicly. You must understand how this works. Contacts tell me that such and such is available for sale. Someone will arrange for me to evaluate the article or articles. At the same meeting, not at some subsequent encounter and after deliberation with other experts, I'm expected to provide a buying price. The possessor doesn't want to get caught with stolen artifacts and is motivated get them off his hands immediately. Usually, he'll take a reasonable price. If I don't meet his expectations, he'll take his wares elsewhere. Or he may lose control of the merchandize to another dealer. That's why my exchanges must be swift and decisive. The cash must be delivered from a private Beirut bank within 24 hours. Otherwise, anything may happen. I'm dealing with fluid situations that come alive and die within hours."

"And you make the final determination to the authenticity of the articles?" asked England from the British Museum.

"There's no time for lengthy evaluation and confirmation."

"And do you have expert assistance?"

"No, only my own experience. I would love to have time for considered opinions and to consult with others. But there is no alternative except to make quick judgments, hopefully the right ones. I must warn you; there's no guarantee I'm right. So far, I'm doing well, but my luck or my judgment might change."

America re-entered, "A blank check for cash to be wired to Beirut, as we did with the last shipment, all based upon your sole judgment! That's asking a lot, isn't it?"

"You've already done it with the last shipment, costing you less than four million American dollars. It worked out well, didn't it?"
"We were testing," answered a respondent who Kar'ine couldn't identify.

"And are you pleased with the test?"
"Could be a scam to trick us into providing much larger sums. We might send buckets of money to Beirut and in return we'd get a condolence note. *Sorry, all funds withdrawn.*"

Kar'ine's head wagged under her *hijab*. She said no more than a single word: "Yes."

"That's a lot of trust. Could be an expensive swindle," said the delegate from the Metropolitan in New York.

Again Kar'ine. "Yes. You may know someone who operates differently. Events in Syria are changing rapidly and the players are constantly in flux. If you can think of a better modus operandi, be my guest."

"Your fee is flexible also, I presume," another unidentified voice.

"No," snapped Kar'ine without hesitation. "I take twenty percent for all trades, delivered. The fee is taken out at the beginning. If the articles are not delivered to Beirut, my entire fee is refunded. From Beirut, the responsibility shifts to the new owners. As in the past, you are required to provide insurance once the artifacts reach the Lebanese capital."

"Why such a high fee?"

"How much is a life worth? It must be worth my while. You'll have to decide whether you wish to continue with me. But you haven't got much time. There are very significant artifacts from Palmyra and Aleppo coming to market soon. To hesitate is to lose."

The delegate from Los Angeles said, "You understand that we cannot provide a *carte blanche* at this moment. We must evaluate the situation before responding. The money is not ours."

"In order not to miss opportunities in Palmyra I must be back in Damascus by Thursday. And that includes travel from Europe in order to re-enter Syria. You'll have to decide quickly if you wish to be players in the upcoming sale. Or find yourselves another broker."

The conference ended in a sour silence, far short of the financial commitment she desired. But at the same time the museum collectors had not given her a definite no. Moments later the video screen shut down.

Porcupine ushered Kar'ine from the conference room and along a stairway that eventually debouched in the museum exhibitions. Their nerves on edge, a heated verbal exchange broke out. To cool their tempers, Porcupine reluctantly granted Kar'ine 45 minutes to view the museum's collection. Here were remnants of the past she had seen only in libraries and archeology journals. Given the possibility that she might soon be back in her native country it wasn't clear she would have another chance.

While returning to Kibbutz Ha-On by car, Porcupine contracted into his thoughts. But when his vehicle began climbing onto the high ridge over the Sea of Galilee, the government agent returned to conversation with instructions. "You see," he said after popping a hard candy into his mouth, "We purposely selected this kibbutz. We wanted somewhere comfortable for you, but far from places where you might be recognized. I'm asking that you don't leave, even with Itamar, until after we hear from the curators. My guess, the day after tomorrow. If things go as we hope, we'll escort you immediately to Istanbul from where your people will get you back to Damascus. This could happen in hours, not days. So be ready. And most of all, please don't share any of this with Itamar."

She expelled air through her lips, eventually saying "that's not going to be easy. He's been a loyal friend. I wouldn't be here were it not for him."

"I understand. You must take my word that his duties at Director of Antiquities are equally important to anything we might accomplish in Damascus. Iti and I have our differences on just about everything, but I recognize him as an honest policeman who guards our precious treasures. As an aficionado of archeology, you can appreciate why he's so important to us."

"What if he demands to know? I can't lie to him."

Porcupine's Subaru began to level off on the summit providing a panoramic view of the Sea of Galilee. His voice lowered to almost a whisper. "My friend from Syria, you are an Arab woman. You were raised in a culture that is filled with lies—between enemies and friends, between lovers and children. When it comes to withholding certain facts, no one, absolutely no one is more skillful than an Arab woman."

"Your people treated me miserably in Istanbul. An *Arab woman*, as you put it, may know how to prevaricate, but we also know how to remember. And such treatment I won't forget."

"We needed to test you."

"And do you know more about me now?"

Porcupine's car turned into the entrance of Kibbutz Ha-On. "No. Not much. My people are risking as much as the museum curators. This could backfire on all of us."

As she prepared to let herself out the passenger door she threw a teasing smile. "And let me remind you that if I fail in Damascus, they'll rape me before applying tortures specially designed for the female anatomy. Keep that in mind when you evaluate my work. And, of course, my compensation."

* * * * *

Itamar knew that Kar'ine had not ended her business with Porcupine. She had pledged to keep in close touch as he maneuvered through the Israeli bureaucracy on her behalf. But she hadn't. That fortified fears she might change her mind about staying in Israel and take a risk on achieving American citizenship. Having earned rich commissions trading antiquities from Ain Dara Temple and Aleppo suburbs and having achieved financial independence, new opportunities opened for her.

He was surprised by her call to his office in Jerusalem. He recalled the exasperation felt when he saw the mobile phone he had left with her on the bed stand at the kibbutz. It was essential to keep in touch and when she had not taken it with her he feared the worst, but out of the blue she was calling him!

"Thank God," he exclaimed. "I returned to the kibbutz but you were gone. Where the hell have you been?"

"With Porcupine."

"That bastard! He promised me he wouldn't talk with you without me present. Promises from him are like treaties to Adolf Hitler. Mere paper to be torn up. I can't tell you how worried I've been. Where are you now?"

"Back on the kibbutz. I've got nothing to do but wait until you visit me. Will that happen?"

"Yes, of course. But first I must know where Porcupine took you. And why."

This was a question she didn't want to answer, however expected. Fortunately, she had rehearsed a fictional response to avoid revealing her conversation with American and European museum curators. "I don't know exactly where. Porcupine asked me to wear an *abaya*. Imagine how foolish I felt. I'm a modern Muslim woman but never in my life felt compelled to cover my flesh. It wasn't mandatory, but I wanted to cooperate. They put a blindfold over my eyes. Where we went is a mystery. Associates in his bureau were not pleased with what I was prepared to tell them. They're asking for more than I can give about my associates."

"Was it in Tell Aviv?"

"Maybe. The route was curvy at first, then straightened out. We ascended into the mountains and after that descended for some time. The return drive was in reverse."

"Did they threaten you?"

Her voice lowered a bit in a moment of hesitation. "No. They were gentlemen who pressed me while at the same time remaining naïve about how I operate."

"Porcupine had no right. I promise you it won't happen again, Kar'ine. I have strong contacts in the highest offices of government who will listen to me."

"It's okay, Itamar. No damage done. Just come to see me."

"How about tomorrow night? I'll take you into Tiberius for dinner. You need an Israeli dinner along the water promenade."

"Sounds delightful. Porcupine told me that for a while I should remain inconspicuous. Not to leave Ha-On."

"You'll be in my custody not his. It's not a bad idea to keep out-of-sight. I'll get women in the kibbutz to lend you some of their clothing for dinner. Would you feel bad by shedding the *hijab* for a single night?"

"Absolutely not. It's only a matter of time when shedding it will be necessary. A restaurant in Tiberius would be a treat. I don't think that Allah will strike me down for abandoning headwear in the Jewish homeland. In Muslim lands, it might be different." She released a characteristic girlish giggle, "It's not clear to me how your Jewish god operates here."

"A puzzle for me, too."

* * * * *

The sun had long since dipped below the western hills bordering the Sea of Galilee, leaving behind a humid, sultry night. The deck lights of small fishing craft reflected on the calm water. The purr of its tiny engine could be heard in the distance. At the waterfront restaurant called *Meracheffit al Pnai Ha Mayim* (Flickering over the Surface of the Water) Itamar and Kar'ine were seated at an outdoor table where a thick candle released a sweet Marigold perfume into the night air. The obligatory hummus and pita began their meal, followed by an array of Israeli salads, none of which were foreign to either Kar'ine or Itamar.

As Itamar regarded the softness of Kar'ine's features through the candlelight it was difficult for him to conjure up how she had endured in Syria. *One tough lady*, he kept repeating to himself. A coping creature who knew how to maneuver in hostile surroundings. Once their business in Istanbul concluded they might have gone in different paths. But their friendship persisted. And now he found this admirable woman in his own country sharing a moment of serenity. Dressed in kibbutz khaki clothing and without her perennial *hijab* she appeared both exotic and familiar.

Dining on Galilee carp, they spoke about her future in Israel. Itamar had made inquiries at the Hebrew University and the Israel Museum about teaching posts in respective departments of antiquities. He could vouch for her expertise in Syrian archeology, a field which most Israeli scholars shunned. The fact that such inquiries were being made by the Director of Israel Antiquities carried heavy weight since nobody in the field wanted to alienate a powerful leader who controlled a substantial government budget.

Conversation flowed easily between them without pause. They had many memories to share and a future to dream about. This was the first time since her arrival in Israel he had observed Kar'ine when not under stress. She seemed relaxed by the quiet ambiance of the night sea. He enjoyed allowing his eyes to settle gently on the soft features of her face, thinking to himself what a magnificent treasure he had found in Istanbul.

Eventually her eyes dropped to the tabletop and she fell into a silence of distant thought. It was his fingers touching hers that brought her back to the moment as she lifted her eyes upon him and said in a subdued voice, "I want you to know, Itamar, that I once met your Gabrielle."

That was a surprise to him. He knew from their days in Istanbul that she had seen Gabby's photograph on his hotel bed stand. He also knew that Gabby had come to Istanbul looking for him. By the time she discovered where he was staying he had left the Turkish capital. "How is that possible?"

A wide smile enlarged Kar'ine cheeks, acknowledging that there were things that even the well-informed Itamar Arad didn't know. "When your Gabrielle was searching for you we met in the shop of Korkut Murat in the Istanbul bazaar. She was posing as an American dealer in the antiquities trade who represented wealthy buyers from Chicago. Korkut Murat told her that I was a seller of Syrian artifacts and he arranged for us to rendezvous in his shop. I figured out pretty fast that she wasn't a dealer. She told me that she was looking for a trader of archeological artifacts who perfectly fit your description. I put two and two together."

"How did your meeting with her end?" he inquired, wishing to conceal how matters between himself and Gabby had gone afoul.

"Badly, I'm afraid," she answered. "It was only three days after we spent that marvelous night in bed with each other. When I realized who she was, I was overwhelmed with grief for having wronged her. In fact the moment I saw her I had the unusual feeling that I was looking not at a rival for your affections but at a sister. I knew then that we both shared the same wonderful thing. My heart broke. How could a decent human being do that to another woman? You know what I did, Itamar?"

Dumfounded by Kar'ine's revelation he just stared forward.

"I fled from Korkut Murat's shop. Can you imagine this self-assured, always composed Kar'ine Salik running away from another woman? But I did. I ran, my eyes clouded by tears. I especially remember the tears because I crashed into a stand of flowers overturning many pots. The crowded pathway was strewn with my clumsiness."

This was completely new to him. Not at all what he might have imagined.

"I would like to meet your Gabrielle again. I knew then what a special person she is. Women have a sense about other women and I never doubted she knew what had occurred between us."

Itamar's lips remained tight but his head wagged in disbelief as Kar'ine continued, "I've told you that my husband had many lovers, and when we were still a couple I hated them all. Between the sheets of my own bed with my husband not one of these women thought about the shame she inflicted upon his wife. And yet...," she paused again, "In your hotel bed I brought equal shame to Gabrielle. I was no better than any of my husband's paramours. Allah will punish my sin."

"No, I cannot accept that," Itamar came alive, "there was no sin in our union. I knew very well the sequence of events that compelled you. No, it was honest and without sin. Neither your Allah nor my Elohim, if either exists, will misunderstand. God put the urge to couple in our bodies; we only responded to His endowment."

"It's more complicated than that, Itamar. I know you think less of me for sleeping with my clients in Damascus. I wouldn't have admitted that to anyone but you. I felt you deserved to know. Understand that sleeping with fellow dealers was nothing like what happened between us. I let them enter between my legs for business only, not for lust and certainly not for love. Only fellow Syrians know what it's like to have one's nation destroyed by civil war. When destruction came to Allepo I knew I needed to rely upon my own resources. I trusted no one until I met you. It is now between me and Allah."

"Gabby and I have had a major falling out," he nearly whispered. "We were a couple until a few days ago. Our differences had absolutely nothing to do with you, Kar'ine. Absolutely nothing. They were entirely professional."

"Do I dare ask what happened?"

"I would tell you, but I cannot. What divided us deals with Israel's state security law. The fact is, I don't even know where Gabby is at the moment."

"Will you get together again?"

"I don't know."

"Do you want to?"

"I don't know that either. Events are moving fast. I need to slow down."

Dinner ended with a quiet stroll along the boardwalk. Words became heavy and therefore it was easier to say nothing. When they arrived at the end of the boardwalk, they turned and walked back in the opposite direction. This occurred twice. Neither wanted to end the night. As they eventually turned toward the direction of the parking lot, she closed the space between them and planted an affectionate kiss upon his cheek. "Thanks for the wonderful meal, Itamar. I haven't enjoyed an evening like this in years. I want you to know that in my prayers I will pray for your reunion with Gabrielle."

"Why would you want to do a thing like that?" he showed his surprise.

Kar'ine didn't have to think about the response that rolled off the tongue, "She's my sister, isn't she. We've both won and then both lost the same thing."

* * * * *

Kar'ine was astonished when Porcupine texted her that the American and European curators had agreed to her terms for purchasing Syrian artifacts, including her uncompromised demand for a 20% commission. She suspected but did not know for certain that Mossad had vouched for her integrity and skill. What she had not considered was that Mossad operated with strict financial controls and that the International Museum Consortium had demanded the Government of Israel guarantee for losses over ten million dollars. Mossad had requested this from the government and, from secret legislation known only to a limited number of officials, the guarantee became a reality. Nothing more than a guarantee, though in this case a guarantee proven to be golden.

No explanation was provided for the Consortium's decision to risk considerable funds other than a concurrence of interests. Kar'ine read through the lines. The press had convinced its American and European readers that the Islamic Republic represented among other things a barbarian upheaval of raw hatred for non-Muslim relics. The art world in America and Europe believed (for right or wrong) that treasures from Syrian history reminded these fanatics that their brand of extremism was incomplete and that they were divinely commanded to destroy artifacts of ancient history, particularly those that predate the Muslim Era. Yet, however destructive, radical Islamists were not entirely mad.

While revolutionary leaders appeared to have little fondness for the past, they recognized that archeological treasures commanded high prices on international markets. And equally important, their revolution proved to be expensive. That realization created a perfect niche for Kar'ine's talents. In the Islamic world the sale of state property was technically a crime and subject to execution. But in the same unforgiving world where misbehavior was treated with ruthless cruelty, Islamic leaders enjoyed many privileges, the most important of which was to acquire personal wealth.

The art of smuggling crafted to a refined degree in the Arab world was perfect for the antiquities trade. The trick Kar'ine employed was to protect her treasure sellers by executing sales quickly for immediate cash, leaving behind no paper trail. And for this she used professional contacts made during her previous life married to a powerful Aleppo curator and past cabinet minister. Most important was a banking relationship with the private Bemo Bank in Beirut where she deposited into a personal account every penny of the monies forwarded by American and European buyers. Only when millions were safely deposited and could be converted to immediate cash would she agree to purchase what Syrian dealers wanted to sell.

Her modus operandi was streamlined. Sellers would present her with I-Phone pictures of what they possessed, along with whatever provenance was known. Kar'ine employed her academic training and personal experience to make snap judgments. Not all her decisions proved perfect, still she reckoned to be ahead if the majority were. If she believed she could purchase for a price acceptable to the Consortium she would order the artifacts brought to the bazaar in the center of Damascus where merchants of every kind were constantly moving merchandise through bustling crowds of shoppers. She rented from Hamid Mustabla, a local shop owner and dealer of electronics, a cubbyhole designed for sipping strong Turkish coffee and haggling. And there, wearing a simple gray robe and her hair mostly covered by a black hijab, she met sellers or their agents. Her trading skill was augmented by a personal rule to raise a bid only once. She understood well how bargaining represented more than negotiating for a favorable price. In Arab culture such haggling was nothing short of traditional sport where buyers and sellers exercised their skills in ongoing haggling, usually extending negotiations over a long period. Kar'ine took control of the timing by moving faster than expected. Since the bulk of the articles she bought was either stolen by thieves or seized by corrupt government officials, speed was critical. Her trump card was the overnight delivery of cash in the form of $100 American bills from the Bemo Bank.

On special occasions, she would agree to spend the night with unmarried or widowed sellers only in an executive suite of the five-star Omayyad Hotel. Elderly men past their sexual prime were the easiest to satisfy. Servicing them usually amounted to little more than cuddling naked under the sheets and fondling their genitals. While in bed in the wee hours of morning, money and artifacts transferred between Aleppo, Damascus and Beirut.

To move her purchases required three Hezbollah transfer agents whom she had come to know through her late spouse. Though they often protested how they worked entirely out of loyalty to her deceased husband, she knew this to be salesmen's' puffery. Half of the 20% commission she charged the Consortium went to those moving her purchases to Beirut.

With two exceptions, all her purchases arrived at their final destinations. Because she personally assumed the financial consequences for these losses, a 4th Century bronze bust from Irbil and a crucifix from a 14th Century Byzantium Church in Aleppo proved to be a financial blow. Since her clients in the United States never paid for these lost artifacts they never learned what they had missed. As far as they knew Kar'ine's record was flawless.

A realist, she always knew that her luck would eventually run thin. And it did, with the arrival of Sheik Saran Piling, a fellow antiquities dealer, to Hamid Mustabla's shop in the Damascus bazaar. The moment she laid eyes upon him she recognized but could not identify someone from her married life. The officiousness of this peddler set a bad tone from the beginning, and she immediately judged his sales pitch to be the product of a fertile imagination. With him were three objects, a 12th Century silver chalice from ruins at Al-Kahf near Margat, a six centimeter cuneiform Babylonian tablet from Ebla and a pottery urn with an impressive provenance originating from Assyrian excavations at Idlib. Kar'ine was interested in the cuneiform tablet and the urn, but not at the prices asked.

In the privacy of Hamid Mustabla's cubicle, she allowed her hijab to settle back on the crown of her head, exposing most of her chestnut brown hair with a tinge of red in the focused electrical lighting. Both dealers sipped sweet tea delivered by a boy who supplied merchants in neighboring shops.

"We have outstanding business between us," announced Saran Piling, "I mean business between your husband and me. He bought two pieces of mine," and here he fetched from an internal pocket a folded paper on which were photocopies of a limestone relief featuring a Silk Road camel caravan and an early Neolithic statue of an earth-mother and her lion cub children, both of which Kar'ine immediately recognized. "Your husband took possession with a promise to pay within a week. Government agents arrested him and he never did. The price for both was $614,000 American. When the police arrested him they returned immediately to your villa where much of his collection was housed. My relief and statue were gone. I'm here to demand that you either pay the money owed or return of my treasures."

Kar'ine's adrenalin surged. Both the relief and statue were among the valuables she had taken with her from Aleppo and later sold in Istanbul. Both hands gripped for her hijab to reposition it forward and disguise a flush in her cheeks. Until that moment she had no reason to believe that in the chaotic establishment of an Islamic caliphate anyone had remembered her husband's private collection. Obviously, she had miscalculated. Under normal circumstances she would immediately returned Saran's possessions, but under pressing conditions in which she needed cash they had been sold in Istanbul for a good deal less than he quoted.

She responded, mustering a confidence she didn't feel, "My husband ran his own affairs, of which he told me nothing. I am very sorry for what you tell me, Saran Piling, but what can I do? Have you taken your claim to the police?"

"You know I can't do that," he was emphatic. "At best they will confiscate whatever I manage to reclaim. My recourse is with you, Kar'ine Salik. Many things went missing from your husband's collection just when you fled to Turkey. If I report what I know to the authorities you're finished in our trade, that is, if you manage to avoid prison. Or worse. A beautiful woman like you will not be underutilized, if you understand my meaning."

Kar'ine fought to control mounting anger that she had become quite adept at doing. She eventually said in a stern voice, "Am I being shaken down by a petty crook, Sheik Saran Piling?"

"I resent that. I am an honest businessman. It's easy for people like you who have fled Syria. You people have left to make new lives abroad. But for those of us forced to remain here life has become very difficult. My family and I have lost everything. When I learned that Dr. Salik had been arrested and later, that he had been tortured and perished, I believed I had lost everything. Then I learned that you were buying here. I don't like threatening you, Kar'ine Salik. I never did business with your husband on that basis. And he never threatened me. But now, I have no alternative."

"I don't have that kind of money."

"Oh, horse shit, Kar'ine Salik. You are dealing here for goods far more valuable than mine. Everybody knows how fast you pay for purchases. Money is easy for you."

"It's not mine, sir. It belongs to my clients. I am only a dealer authorized to buy for them, not on my own account."

He emitted an artificial grin. "Of course. But you are a trained accountant by trade, an expert with numbers. You could shift funds to your own account. You're far from your principles. Nobody would know the difference."

Her head bobbed in approval. "Of course I could do something like that, but I am telling you I shall not. I enjoy a sacred trust with my clients."

"And business between your husband and me? Was that not a sacred trust, too?"

"I could manage some personal funds for you but only a fraction of the sum you seek."

"How much?"

"I must consult with my bank in Beirut."

"Do that. You know I always envied Dr. Salik. I was particularly jealous of him for his able and exceptionally beautiful wife. War brings strange consequences. To think that I am now in the presence of this same striking woman, demanding from her…"

"I'm sorry what happened with my husband. I am not responsible for his misdeeds. And I'm warning you now that I can assume only a token of your losses. As you say, war causes unforeseen consequences. You'll have to be satisfied with less than a full loaf."

* * * * *

Father Sebastian Alejandro was a monkish Bethlehem friar who had taken sanctuary in the minutia of New Testament scholarship. He stood no more than 1.5 meters high, and, as his colleagues at the École Biblique et Archéologique were constantly reminding him, he was 40 pounds overweight. Curiosity about events of the past kept him out-of-touch with all but selected churchmen who believed that by ferreting out textual truths about the life of their Savior they personally narrowed the distance to this Heavenly Deity.

For 23 years his work at the Ecole had been mentored by the late Father Dr. Benoir Matteau, the Ecole's eccentric and often tyrannical Director of Field Archeology. But since Benoir's mysterious death in the Judean Desert, Father Sebastian found himself abandoned to his own resources without guidance or inspiration. After Benoir's demise, Sebastian lost his concentration. Projects he had begun during his teacher's life floundered, giving rise to a relentless depression. He was aware that Benoir's death left other scholars languishing, but they were members of a closed-mouth brotherhood who seldom spoke about personal feelings. Without strong leadership, the once ebullient enthusiasm of the Ecole never returned.

The fact that Brother Benoir died intestate, without a will for the distribution of his worldly effects, rescued Sebastian from a precipitous descent into total abandonment. Because everyone at the Ecole knew of his special attachment to the deceased, the new Acting Director appointed him Benoir Matteau's executor. That meant gathering the dead priest's meager possessions. An easy task, but sorting out a messy collection of scholarly papers and archeological notes proved to be far more challenging.

Unbeknown to the faculty at the Ecole, Sebastian also began adding to and editing Benoir's unfinished notes. Two of his unpublished monographs, one on the disciple Simon and the other the tormented Judas, made it into prestigious New Testament journals. Though Sebastian had done 90% of the work, he assumed a modest third position among a long string of contributing authors.

And then this Dominican priest-scholar stumbled into a series of almost illegible notes and memoirs hidden in a closet by Father Benoir. Here Sebastian believed he possessed a unique advantage over his colleagues. Only someone who had toiled with Benior so closely for so many years was equipped to decipher an almost illegible script. What the brethren believed to be penmanship crippled by Benoir's advancing Parkinson's disease he discovered to be a private script. This in Sebastian's mind had to be deliberate stratagem meant to hide critical data from those who might misunderstand or misuse it.

Deciphering these memoirs provided Sebastian with a new lease on life, joining him once again with the professional companion who gave substance to his own scholarly inquiries. During an interlude of discovery in which Sebastian could think of nothing but Benoir's notes, he abandoned camaraderie at the Ecole, avoiding communal meals and daily walks with friends around Bethlehem's squares. His withdrawal into the dark world of his deceased teacher proved to be enormously intriguing.

To understand these notations, he also abandoned the Ecole to retrace his mentor's footsteps through the Promised Land, ever searching for clues to unravel the deceased priest's thoughts. His travels eventually brought him to Sodom on the southern lip of the Dead Sea where he learn that an American production company was making a documentary about the late Professor Timothy Matternly, Benoir's accomplice in rescuing fragments from Cave XII at Qumran. It was not so much the document makers that interested him as Gabrielle Lewyn, an established expert on the discoveries of Timothy Matternly and the Senior Curator of the Matternly Collection at the Shrine of the Book in Jerusalem.

* * * * *

A steady stream of journalists arrived at Warpath Enterprises' temporary headquarters in Sodom, searching for Dr. Gabrielle Lewyn. There, they were turned away and advised to make contact with her at the Shrine of the Book in Jerusalem. The same response was given to Father Sebastian when he showed up at Warpath's rented quarters attired in the threadbare and sun-bleached tunic of a desert vagabond. When turned away by a Warpath employee, the portly Dominican became skeptical, reckoning that since Gabrielle Lewyn was critical to a documentary about Timothy Matternly she had to be nearby. It was only a matter of time before she was certain to emerge, and he was prepared to wait.

Like Benoir, he loved tramping along biblical pathways. Knowing what was published about the discoveries of Cave XII and the school for prophets at Ein Arugot, there were several locations he intended to visit. These days tourists visiting Qumran were transported in air-conditioned buses. But he preferred following ancient footpaths on foot, imagining himself trekking alongside his biblical ancestors.

From a meager monthly allowance Sebastian rented a tiny room perched on the hillside above the hostel where Lydia Browner housed the Warpath staff. Like Father Benoir who continuously surrounded himself with beautiful women to test his celibacy, Sebastian enjoyed observing women through binoculars, not as a sexual voyeur but as a student of the feminine form. From the window of his rented room he watched the Warpath girls come and go throughout the day. One Shabbat morning he witnessed four ladies pile into their battered Korean van and head down the mountainside to the Dead Sea shore. By their skimpy outfits he assumed they planned to bathe in the Sea.

In the boredom of Shabbat when almost everything in Israel slows to a sleepy standstill, Sebastian followed the ladies on foot. During past years access to the saline waters had diminished as fresh water feeding the Dead Sea from the Galilee was diverted for agricultural purposes. The Warpath women did not bathe with other tourists and patients seeking relief from psoriasis on one of the remaining beaches, but motored further south to an isolated stretch of shoreline.

On foot, it took him almost an hour in beating sun to catch up. Keeping out of sight, he observed the women cluster on a shallow sandbar where to his surprise they had abandoned all clothing and had waded naked into the water. The hyper-saline liquid forced their bodies to float on the surface. To avoid salt in their eyes they turned on their backs, immodestly exposing to the sun the entire lengths of their flesh. He couldn't pretend that he wasn't aroused. But, like his mentor Brother Benoir, he believed a priest must honor his vows of celibacy and that meant avoiding arousal. This forced him to lift his eyes from this erotic scene to study natural sandstone sculptures populating the rocky hillside.

Where he sat there was no shade from the blistering sun. For relief, he approached the water where he slipped out of his tunic and, retaining his sandals waded in, immediately floating to the surface. His feet displayed a row of stubby but straight toes popping to the surface. The salt-rich water heated by a blazing sun warmed his flesh.

By the time he waded to the shore, the women further along the beach had already dressed and were gathering their belongings to climb back to their van parked on the roadway above. Sebastian knew it was time to retreat from the sun, but as he was dressing dizziness overwhelmed him. He staggered and, for a brief moment, his legs gave way under him. It was only momentary, but one of the women climbing the hill must have noticed and shifted her trajectory along the stony embankment to be of assistance.

"Too much sun," she called out as she approached with a plastic bottle of water in hand. At the moment Sebastian had just dipped his head under a silver chain with the holy cross of his Savior and settled it upon his shoulders.

"Are you alright?" a lean, well-proportioned woman asked. "Oh, Father," she corrected having seen that he was a member of the clergy.

"Of course," he responded, straightening up to study the features of his rescuer. He replaced round spectacles over his ears and squinted in the sunlight. When his vision cleared he said, "I know you, don't I?"

"I don't think so," she replied.

He chuckled aloud which expanded into a gagging series of laughs that for a moment was uncontrollable.

"Excuse me," she interjected. "Have I missed something? I think I put all my clothes back on, or have I forgotten something essential?"

"No, most certainly not." He stopped laughing long enough to say, "I'm laughing because I've come from Bethlehem to Sodom to talk with you and your friends said you were not here. You're Rabbi Lewyn, aren't you? It never occurred to me that I'd meet you at the waterside. But I do want to speak with you."

"How did you know I'd be here?" she inquired attempting to hide her skepticism.

"I didn't know for sure. I knew about a documentary being made and I took a chance. Frankly, I had no other choice. And by the way, I'm Father Sebastian Alejandro, a student and colleague of the late Father Benoir Matteau. You know him, of course?"

She hadn't heard Father Benoir's name for many months, but of course she knew him. Quite well, as a matter of fact. This was a memory that she didn't wish to encourage. "Yes," she responded and then said nothing more.

"I must talk with you, Rabbi. I have information that will interest you. It deals with Father Benoir's work. I know he had a falling out with Professor Matternly."

Lydia's women were calling from the roadside for Gabby to join them for a ride back to their quarters. "I can't talk now," she added. "I'm amazed that you found me."

"Can we talk this evening? You've done the primary work on Reverend Matternly's discoveries. I've brought you information about Benoir Matteau you won't learn elsewhere." Gabby thought fast and came up with the only solution that occurred to her. "This evening at the bar of the Sheraton Hotel. Say 8:30. I'll be on the banquet against the back wall. Father, if you wish to speak with me you must keep this secret. These are hard times for me. I'm not eager to be seen in public."

Sebastian revealed a mouth of decent but not perfect yellowish teeth. His puffy face opened into an engaging smile. "You have my word. And you won't be disappointed. 8:30 at the Sheraton. In the bar. At the rear."

* * * * *

Being tardy for a meeting was not customary for Gabby. But to rendezvous with Father Sebastian at the appointed time she was forced to climb the hillside to the hotel, a distance which she had underestimated. In the Sheraton bar, she found the priest already seated opposite the banquet with his back toward the door. A black robe of the Dominican order was draped over his shoulders, above which lay a black and white *kafia*, traditional headgear for Jordanian Arabs. A tumbler half-filled with what looked to be Scotch was in his fist, and when he turned to acknowledge Gabby moist eyes peering through round spectacles told her that the alcohol had already taken effect.

She dropped beside him onto the empty banquet, careful to hide her face from public view. A friendly pat on the cleric's shoulder established her comfort with the Catholic clergyman. It wasn't clear that he felt equally comfortable with her. Their conversation opened with banter about the heat and the utter desolation of Sodom, not a place where either of them wished to remain long.

She eventually turned the conversation to what was primary in her mind. "What you told me on the beach was intriguing. You probably know that Benoir Matteau and I were not friends."

"Of course, but that was when Cave XII was originally robbed, but now…" and here Sebastian revealed the full range of his teeth in a broad smile, "things have changed. I would guess that today you and Benoir would share a common point of view. Unfortunately, the poor man came to an untimely death. You might be aware that when a priest dies there isn't always a family to administer his unfinished business, such as estates and legacies. Father Benoir was a loner. If he had a family he never spoke about it. He had numerous professional associates, men like Professor Matternly, but very few friends. I loved him dearly, but in truth I don't believe he ever loved me back. Oh yes, he helped me in my profession. Scholar clerics are not like other priests. If we don't produce worthy scholarship we're shifted into parish work. Not a career change that any of us aspired to. Father Benoir saw to it that I was always productive. We were never intimate friends. There were rumors that we were more than professional colleagues, but I can assure you that was never, never true. When he died without a will the Ecole's Acting Director needed someone to administer his final estate. I volunteered. That's how I found his memoirs."

Gabby ordered a Goldstar beer from a pudgy Palestinian waiter who appeared indifferent to waiting on tables. Gabby remained dubious about Sebastian's speculation that her relationship with Benoir would have improved over time. She had pieced together enough of the saga about Tim Matternly and Father Benoir to understand how they violently clashed over possession of the *Yeshu* Fragment. Details of this conflict she never learned fully.

Sebastian waited until the Palestinian unceremoniously deposited a bottle of beer before Gabby and before asking if he wanted another whiskey rushed away from the banquet. The priest let him go. "For a year I have been trying to get a report on Father Benoir's death from the Israel police. They told me that the delay was solely bureaucratic, but I don't believe them. I have reason to think that Father Benoir was murdered not far from here. Bedouins were involved, but they often work for the Jewish police. So as far as the police are concerned no murder ever occurred."

Gabby had long understood that both Timothy and Benoir were slain where Bedouin tended their flocks. A single police account attributed Tim's death to a tribal conflict.

But Benoir was a different story. The last official record of his presence was in the Vatican. Bullshit! Gabby had seen Benoir in Jerusalem's Old City. She told that to the police, but nothing came of it. The police said there was no official record of Benoir having re-entered Israel from Italy. And no Israeli policeman in his right mind would investigate the death of someone who wasn't even in the country. Gabby suspected that Father Sebastian had not come all the way from Bethlehem to voice his speculations about Benoir's death. While her curiosity was stirred, she did not know the priest well enough to steer him forward. It was clear he was enjoying alcoholic beverages and perhaps to a lesser extent her company.

Sebastian took a long swallow from the last of his scotch and, observing that he had drained the glass, snapped his fingers to signal for a refill. Gabby waved her arm to attract the waiter's attention. "You see," began the priest, "I got excited when I recently saw the name *Yeshu* on YouTube. You saw this, of course?"

"Yes. Absolutely." she said. "It came out of the wind, as a total surprise."

"Well, you see, it wasn't the fragment that surprised me because I already knew it existed."

"God told you, perhaps?" she hid her curiosity in thick sarcasm.

"No. I learned of the fragment from Father Benoir's notes. In his diary chronicling events around Cave XII he wrote about the proper name of our Lord Jesus on a parchment fragment. And he also wrote that he and Professor Matternly quarreled over it. I must tell you what you may not like hearing. At one point Brother Benoir wrote that your friend the professor *stole* the *Yeshu* Fragment from him."

None of that surprised Gabby though it did make her more curious about what Sebastian knew.

"Benoir's notes talk of three trips to the Monastery of St. George near Jericho where Professor Matternly was scanning the fragments they had jointly removed from Cave XII. The notes say that Benoir returned to Bethlehem while Matternly remained in the monastery. It appears they never questioned that, by law, everything taken from the cave belonged to the Government of Israel. But Benoir didn't get along well with your friend, Dr. Itamar Arad. He felt Arad's Department of Antiquities favored Israeli over Church scholars and equally important he was impatient to work on what he and Matternly took from Cave XII. Father Benoir feared his failing health would prevent him from investigating these new documents. Still, he conceded to Matternly that as soon as they had scanned the fragments, they would turn over all the originals to the Israel Antiquities Authority. Sale of these invaluable documents was never discussed. Their primary interest was to study, not to own or sell. Scans and photocopies would serve their scholarly purposes.

Sebastian's narrative triggered in Gabby many memories of the events before the *Yeshu* Fragment was traded with the Vatican. There were many lacunae in the story she had patched together. Sebastian was filling in.

She interjected into the conversation, "The Monastery of St. George is new to me. It makes sense that since Tim had developed software for deciphering fragmented documents he would take responsibility for the scanning. You know about the software he developed at the University of Chicago, don't you?"

"Who doesn't? Matternly was a pioneer. Of course, there's an improvement in the code these days, but when it was developed nobody believed Matternly's work was possible."

"If you've written down what you just told me, I'd love to review the entirety of Father Benoir's notes. They'd be essential for the collection at the Shrine of the Book."

Sebastian rubbed the flesh on his neck that had begun to transition into a double chin. "Father Benoir and I passed many hours together. Before he was summoned to Rome, we spent leisure time in Jerusalem bars. He liked to invite attractive women to join us. Not unpleasant for me, you should know. Sometimes he became a little tipsy which I found strange for a man of his discipline."

Sebastian paused to study ice in his glass before coaxing from the liquid remains a scotch flavor. In a lower voice he almost whispered, "The Israel government has just denied the *Yeshu* Fragment on YouTube and called it a hoax. I noticed that you did not participate in this denunciation. Your opinion would have been valuable but you were silent. There must be a reason."

She nodded agreement, determined not to disclose her personal differences with Itamar. The priest had no need to know about her interview with Prime Minister Sonnenberg.

"What disturbed me," he continued his own thread of thought, "was not what Jewish scholars said but the response in Rome. Vatican authorities were as vehement in their denunciation as Jerusalem. Still there's a major difference between them. I'm unsure what Jerusalem knows, but I'm certain that Rome is lying. Father Benoir went to Rome to explain his discovery. He must have told Church scholars about the fragment. In my opinion Rome has always known. And if Rome knows the Holy Father knows."

Sebastian paused to evaluate the effect of his disclosure upon Gabby who struggled to suppress her lack of surprise. She agreed with all that he said. In fact, nothing was new, except for one thing—the *Yeshu* Fragment must have been mentioned in Benoir's notes. How else would Father Sebastian know the YouTube fragment was genuine? And if that were true, it would prove beyond a doubt that her Xerox copy was a duplicate of the original document.

"So, you believe the YouTube entry isn't a fake?" asked Gabby.

"No question. It's genuine. My guess, you've known this all along. Yes?"

She executed an ambiguous nod and filled the momentary silence with, "What do you plan to do with these notes, Father?"

A hand slipped into his tunic and rummaged for an internal pocket. It was withdrawn a moment later to pat an external side pouch. The priest's frustration was apparent. Both hands dropped to his trousers and forcefully probed. The cleric's face flushed red and she noted a slight quiver in his upper lip. "I've brought you some of Benoir's transcribed notes. On a computer memory stick. But…but it seems to have slipped from my pocket. I'm sure I put it into my tunic before leaving this evening. I guess I can make a new copy in Bethlehem, but I wouldn't want someone else to see it. I made it for you only. Because I trust you not to misuse it. These notes should eventually reside in the Shrine of the Book where Father Benoir would have wished them."

Having access to Benoir's notes had not entered her thinking. Impatience overwhelmed her. If Sebastian needed to return to Bethlehem in order to reproduce his memory stick, there was a possibility something might intervene to prevent her from ever seeing the notes. "May I suggest, dear Father, that you search through your pockets once more?"

Sebastian produced a weak smile before immediately standing up and putting his hands back to work, exploring multiple pockets. Nothing turned up until he shifted his weight to accommodate for deeper penetration of his interior pocket. "Voila!" he exclaimed with a flash of toothy victory, fishing out a memory stick. Without ceremony, he pushed it toward Gabby's willing hand.

He sighed audibly and curled his lips before stating, "Rabbi Lewyn, you must be sensitive to politics in the Church. I've spent my career in its service. If I publish these notes, I'm likely to be out in the alleys of Bethlehem. Were I to go public with what I know, the Church will post me to the jungles of Africa. Or worse. Lowly Dominican priests have been known to disappear, just like Father Benoir. But with you that's a different matter. I haven't told anyone until now."

"So why do you trust me?"

"Because whether we are friends or not, we're sailing in the same boat. I don't think you'd be in Sodom if you felt secure in Jerusalem. A confidant told me there are men hunting for you, thugs from Eastern Europe. Professional hit men. You know the expression *hit-men*, don't you?"

That didn't surprise her. She feared that Zebulon Sonnenberg's deputies would be looking to arrest her for a violation of state secrets. But a threat from European thugs, that didn't sound like what she expected from the Prime Minister. In difficult situations Gabby's humor clicked in and for a moment an inner chuckle erupted. For men the *Yeshu* Fragment would be considered a great blessing. But certainly not for her. It had brought with it a curse. And as briefly as her humor arose it disappeared. Suddenly it became a matter of controlling a tremor in her hands, often aggravated by stressful situations.

"So, good Father Sebastian," she stared into alcoholic eyes behind thick spectacles, "where do we go with this knowledge?"

"I was hoping that as a rabbi you might use your contacts to let the world know the truth. You must appreciate that as a priest, I cannot."

"Of course. Do you know who's looking for me?"

He shook his head negatively. "Only that they're the kind of people who get paid to hurt others. Churchmen have learned to defend themselves against such evil people. Some of us are far stronger than laymen believe. It may surprise you to learn that we have guns and we know how to use them. If you need help, Rabbi Lewyn, we will protect you."

The rabbi and priest parted company on a road high over the Dead Sea. Both knew there was much to understand. And for the moment Gabby must now be more cautious than before. Somehow she had managed to get herself between two tigers.

* * * * *

It was well past bedtime by the time Gabby crept into the hostel. This worked to her advantage because she was in no mood to chat with her new roommates, or more accurately, assigned bedmates. Lydia had delegated her to a cubbyhole of a room with two twin beds, leaving barely enough room to walk around. And along with her bed came Gila Tazon, an ex-colonel in the Israel Defense Force and video editor with flaming red hair and a bellowing voice. In the adjoining bed, Claire Gizelforte, a Czechoslovakian sound expert and part-time scriptwriter.

Gabby undressed to her underwear, flossed her teeth and prepared to slip under the covers beside Gila, breathing heavily in a deep sleep. Out of deference for Jewish tradition, she recited the *K'reat Shema*, the last prayer of the day for an observant Jew (which she wasn't), and tried to settle her mind after the day's events.

She had barely advanced into the world of slumber before Gila's lips lightly covered her ears. Along her chest she became aware of warm flesh, with protrusions she recognized as nipples. Between caresses and Hebrew words of affection, words Gabby knew well enough but chose not to answer. The gentleness of Gila's love-making she did not mistake for rape. But it was nevertheless unwanted and certainly unsolicited. She turned her head from Gila muttering that she was in no mood for affection, then onto her side to present her back to this uninvited lover. Undiscouraged, Gila made a second attempt to turn Gabby who now defended herself by pushing forcefully away with her free hand. She was relieved when Gila seemed to accept the rebuff, but come morning they'd have to have a serious talk.

Yet it wasn't that simple. Claire Gizelforte had been awakened by movement in Gabby's bed. She regarded Gila's rejection as an opportunity for herself. Once the sleepers had settled down, Claire alighted from her bed and stepped over to Gabby. Both hands reached out to touch Gabby's cheeks and moved immediately to urge her from Gila's bed to her own. A second seduction, no matter how affectionately offered, tested Gabby's patience. She wrenched free of entanglement by elbowing Claire's hands. The unexpected blow caused Claire to withdraw and, stepping back, whispered, "You must be exhausted; tomorrow night for certain, yes? I catch you when you're not so tired, Love."

Chapter Six

A memo placed in front of him while on his office phone made Itamar's complexion blanch. For a brief moment he experienced a constriction in the veins servicing his wrists and a sharp pain in the left ankle. What wasn't supposed to occur had happened, producing a horrible result, one he believed was certain to tumble him from the antiquities directorship he had come to love.

It started when he accepted a sabbatical position policing antiquities in the Palestine Authority. He didn't have to use this year to help protect Palestinian artifacts, but felt that Israel had a responsibility to share its experience protecting the region's historical past. His professional associates had warned him not to take on a job certain to be filled with both seen and unseen entanglements, as well as Jerusalem and Ramallah politics. Despite such counsel, he bull-headedly assumed the responsibility, confident in his ability to close the theft of Palestinian artifacts. And that, he argued to himself, was to Israel's long-term benefit. First, Palestine's archeological past merged with Israel's archeological history. And vice-versa. And secondly, when Palestinians took pride in their ancient past they would become better neighbors.

And to a reasonable level Itamar succeeded in his goal. All within a single sabbatical year! Almost, but not entirely.

On day one of this new job, he was appalled to learn that unlike the Department of Antiquities in Israel which maintained an accurate register of all historical and archeological artifacts, the equivalent agency, the Palestine Ministry of Culture and Tourism, possessed nothing more than a single cabinet drawer stuffed with 5x7 cards purporting to be an exhaustive catalogue of Palestine's antiquities.

Itamar inherited a mess. Virtually no records, zero policing staff, and a long established history of outright thievery. The political leaders of the Palestine Authority, constantly wrestling with internal political rivalries and Israeli military occupation, had little or no energy left for protecting the nation's past that, lamentably, was slipping out the door day by day. In fact, Itamar discovered that the Authority's governing Fatah party was not only ineffective in preventing theft but often the corrupt beneficiary of such robbery. Arriving in Ramallah on a white stallion to save what was left of Palestinian treasures, Itamar plowed forthright into his job.

First things first, he resolved to get a census of Palestinian antiquities by organizing a credible roster of known and proposed archeological sites. Next came an index of significant artifacts along with their current locations and, where possible, the names and addresses of their possessors, including foreign owners. On the surface it might have seemed uncomplicated but in reality required countless field trips to verify both the current state of past excavations and the actual presence of existing antiquities. And all this understaffed with only three part-time employees! The mission required considerable computational skills with computers that the Palestine Ministry of Culture didn't possess.

When his sabbatical year ended, nobody judged Itamar's tenure a failure. First and foremost he managed to cobble together pieces of bureaucratic chaos and fashioned a small but operating department. Next, he had traveled to Istanbul to discover how archeological treasures were being secreted from Jericho and peddled off to the international trade. Worthy and commendable work, but not what Itamar believed to be his lasting contribution. That turned out to be an official register of Palestinian treasures and their current locations—both known and lost.

Upon returning to Jerusalem, he employed the extensive powers of Israeli computation. The data he had amassed in Palestine required considerable sifting and sorting, all with the talents of his Israeli staff. What resulted was more startling that he had anticipated; the state of Palestine antiquities was far worse than suspected. 68 percent of Palestine's known artifacts were neither in museums or the Authority's archive. And a whopping 54 percent of treasures once in possession of Fatah officials were missing. In the conclusion of his confidential report to the Israeli Cabinet, Itamar wrote an opinion that the current and past leadership of the ruling political party was guilty of grand larceny. Corrupt officials had obviously enriched themselves by selling off Palestine's past.

Itamar's statistics and his conclusions were included in a Final Report, along with instructions to be extremely cautious about publicizing such explosive figures, especially when the current center-right coalition government in Jerusalem enjoyed a less than cordial working relationship with Fatah. No one would say Fatah and Israel were fond bedmates, but unlike the Hamas Party in Gaza, Fatah had produced reasonable leaders who acknowledged the reality of Israeli sovereignty. Before turning over his report to the government Itamar made certain the contents were classified TOP SECRET. That's where he believed his startling observations would end. Nobody in Israel condoned Arab corruption but just about everybody had come to accept it as a functional reality.

But, damn them to hell, somebody in the Cabinet, most probably supporters of the right wing settlers who sought to torpedo a final land distribution between Israelis and Palestinians, leaked the confidential report to the New York Times. It was not the first time such leaks occurred and probably would not be the last. But Itamar was the author of this explosive report and, as such, became an instant target for criticism.

Attached to the memo his associate put on Itamar's desk was a photocopy of the New York Times article. It took him no more than a moment to expect a call from a furious Prime Minister. While the Zebulon Sonnenberg was well acquainted with Israel's sewer politics and would never believe that his Director of Antiquities would leak this report to the press, he was not beyond fingering a scapegoat. Somebody's head would have to roll for the damage the report would do to Israel-Palestine relations and the on-going peace process (at the moment in recess). And who better than Itamar Arad? Kill the Messenger.

But perhaps even more damaging, Itamar had cherished his professional contacts in Ramallah. He had made great effort to nurture friendships, even among those he knew to be involved in illegal sales. Now it was highly questionable if he had any friends left in the Palestine Authority. He knew that embarrassing Palestine politicians was not the way to maintain good working relations and to be invited back by the Palestine Authority. And to travel there now, just a few paces over the Israeli frontier, meant taking his life in his hands.

* * * * *

Father Sebastian Alejandro's computer memory stick, delivered to Gabby, completed a story about which she was a critical player but about which she only knew a part.

From the moment she discovered the *Yeshu* Fragment hidden between the pages of her Kittel Bible in Jerusalem she knew Tim Matternly had put it there. At the time she had not communicated with Tim since his departure from Chicago, except for a brief email claiming to have made a major discovery. All that had transpired between him and Father Benoir she subsequently inferred from a small core of perceived facts. For a start, she knew that Tim had discovered the fragment but not how, that is until she later entered Cave XII with Itamar and found a discarded plastic sandwich bag, the type Tim often used for storing small archeological items. Also, she knew that he had been collaborating with Father Benoir Matteau and that they had a falling out, but not precisely why. Additionally, she knew that most of Tim's discoveries in the form of parchment fragments had been secreted by Benoir from Israel to the Vatican, but not how this feat (some would later call it robbery) had been accomplished.

Father Sebastian's notes on Benoir filled in many historical lacunae. Gabby now turned her thoughts to a new question, why Benoir had found it necessary to keep meticulous notes regarding this venture. One clue, according to Sebastian, was that the priest's notations ranged over a full professional career, and that those relevant to Qurman represented only the most significant portion. Written in nearly illegible handwriting with numerous coded words and undefined symbols, they were probably never intended for others to read. Gabby speculated that as a consummate archeologist trained to take extensive notes on just about everything, he was acting out of professional discipline. Perhaps he planned to unscramble these notes in the future. He, more than academic scholars, understood the significance of the *Yeshu* Fragment for Christian theology, and probably wanted to maintain an historical record for posterity. That he wrote in a private script with personal symbols and references guaranteed his notes would not be misused. That he underestimated the extraordinary devotion and skill of his disciple Sebastian was simply careless thinking.

In the Warpath hostel, Gabby chronicled a time-line of events, conjecturing that Benoir had penned his notes while residing in the Vatican and had brought them to his Bethlehem office during his last visit to the Holy Land. It was possible he planned to edit his notes at a future time, but that will never be known.

What she had come to realize was that while the *Yeshu* Fragment undermined much of convention Christian knowledge about the Savior, the drama of its discovery at Qumran and later the modern conflict between Tim Matternly, a Presbyterian professor, and Benoir Matteau, a Dominican priest, made for compelling drama. That means that the documentary script she had previously sketched out for Lydia Browner had missed the target. Theological speculation was one thing; engaging, compelling drama, quite another.

* * * * *

After patiently hearing Gabby's complaint how she suffered from sleep deprivation fighting off sexual advances by her roommates, Lydia caved in and offered her a cot next to her own bed in the hostel's only private room.

In the desert heat of Sodom, the production team of Warpath had become accustomed to a leisurely siesta after lunch. Lydia was lying under the ceiling fan while Gabby rested on a canvas cot. Lydia wore a sports bra and absolutely nothing more. Gabby had become accustomed to her nudity, joking to herself that were she to possess a sculpted body like that she would become a dedicated nudist herself. At the same time she was acutely aware of how Lydia employed this weapon. Neither male nor females eyes could avoid her. Courteous voyeurs pretended to shift their vision but their eyes immediately returned whenever possible.

"You what?" Lydia almost howled and drew herself into a sitting position when Gabby broached the subject of changing the Matternly script. "You must understand, dear friend, that Warpath is currently insolvent. We've bet the farm on this documentary and if we don't stay on schedule I'll be back on the courts pitching tennis balls to senior citizens in South Florida. You must know I would never bully you, but not only do I not want to revise our script, it can't be done—not without an influx of new money, which I don't have and can't possibly squeeze from my lenders. Not one penny more."

Gabby knew how to be diplomatic by leading a controversial subject with a soft question. "Lydia, tell me what you envision for your film?"

"A wide viewership, of course."

"What if I told you that if you agree to let me change directions you will have the whole American and European audiences in your pocket? Sounds like hyperbole but you know I do not kid."

"You don't kid but you exaggerate, my love."

"Have you ever really heard me exaggerate?"

"Daily, you're God's hyperbole on this fucking lonely planet."

"Untrue. At this moment, I possess a secret that only a very few people know. In archeology it's the most important fact to emerge since the Rosetta Stone. And you, my dear, are poised to become the world's most famous documentarian."

"From anyone but Gabrielle Lewyn, I'd laugh out loud. Tell me what you have in mind."

"I can't until you pledge to turn what I know into your documentary. You'll never regret it."

"On a mere pledge of friendship?"

Gabby paused letting her eyes shift over gentle curves on Lydia's belly, only slight less taught than twenty years before. "Yes. That's exactly what I'm asking. I now know how Tim Matternly discovered the fragments. And the role of the Latin Church in the affair. This will require rewriting to include these facts. And much more."

"Since my coffers are empty, I haven't got funds to change course, even if I were willing, which I'm probably not. Especially since I don't know what you have in mind."

"I promise you I can raise every shekel you'll need, and it will all come back in spades. You'll be a very wealthy woman."

"Sounds great. Let's assume I agree, which I haven't. Now please tell me what I'm asked to agree to."

Gabby held on to her secret until the very last moment, though she knew it was not possible to proceed without revealing it. The secret was in solemn trust with Itamar and, though at the moment she believed that the gag rule no longer governed this secret, she also believed she had never breached a solemn oath. Once the fragment appeared on YouTube it was only a matter of time before the world would come to learn of the secret deal fashioned between the Vatican and the Israel Government.

Gabby maintained silent until Lydia was bound to lose interest. Finally, she said, "Even if you don't agree to make this documentary I need your word not to repeat what I'm about to tell you. Can I count upon you, Lydia?"

"My love, have I ever let you down? I've even kept my hands off you while you slept next to me, defying every hormone in my body."

Gabby breathed heavily, expelling air just before capturing more, as though this might be her last. Lydia's legs suddenly curled over the bed and her feet with freshly painted toenails transferred to the floor. "Wait a second," she exclaimed. "Before you tell me I must put my socks on so you can knock them off. She actually bent over to snatch from under the bed a pair of sweat socks and running shorts. Once she secured the shorts on her hips she dropped down again to the bed. "Ready now," she announced. "Shoot!"

Gabby's voice faltered for a phrase or two before she got into stride, speaking in slow sentences to provide a chronological sequence of events, beginning with the theft of Quran Cave XII by Tim Matternly and Father Benoir Matteau, then moving to the Monastery of St. George where Tim digitalized the stolen fragments. It was there that he stumbled upon a fragment with three Hebrew words, the proper name of Christianity's savior, Jesus, followed by the family identification, "son of Joseph."

Gabby paused to let Lydia ask for clarification, noting that though she professed to be an atheist she wouldn't misunderstand the implication of Tim's discovery for Christian thinking. She read Lydia's brain concentrating not on the implications for Christian theology but on how this might be portrayed in a documentary.

Gabby continued to tell how Father Benoir visited St. George's where Tim shared with him the *Yeshu* Fragment. Benoir believed that this priceless document belonged to the Catholic Church while Matternly wanted to make copies and deliver the original to its lawful owner, the State of Israel. Their partnership unraveled in a vociferous argument.

Lydia's interest sparked. A strong controversy was the ideal stuff for a documentary. She was even more pleased when Gabby told how Tim had taped the fragment to his back and rappelled off the monastery wall at night to make a dash for Jerusalem. The following morning Benoir seized the bulk of the new fragments that he later spirited to Rome aboard a corporate jet dispatched by the Roman Church.

To Lydia's mind, not only was this story explosive, but filled with compelling action in the ancient home of Christian thought. Perfect for a dynamic, action-packed documentary.

Gabby filled in the succeeding story of how Tim had hidden the fragment in a Hebrew volume of the Old Testament in the apartment she shared with him on Jerusalem's Usshishkin Street and, after Tim's murder in the Judean Desert, how she had inadvertently discovered it. Next, came an unpleasant encounter with hired thugs in the employ of Father Benoir. She took it upon herself to see that this historic fragment became the property of the State of Israel. The final chapter was the negotiation with Church officials in Rome, in which the Government of Israel exchanged the *Yeshu* Fragment for the remaining documents and fragments Benoir had stolen and which later became the core collection in the new Timothy Matternly wing of the Shrine of the Book.

"Wow," Lydia exclaimed. "If you can write this script I can capture it, but it's going to take a lot of money. My production team is way too small. How much time do you need?"

"Under normal conditions about three weeks, but nothing's normal these days. Rome thinks I leaked the YouTube video and I've just learned that some nasty people are looking for me. And what's even worse, the Israel Prime Minister thinks I'm responsible for breaking my pledge and is threatening to arrest me for violating state secrets. I can't work here. My new friend, Father Sebastian, has offered to find a safe place for me."

Lydia rose again to reseat herself beside Gabby, lacing her fingers in hers. "My dear Gabby. I've been pursuing you for years. Now that you've shared this secret with me, it's time you came to sleep in my bed. I'm not asking for you to abandon men. God made women like you to sleep out their nights with males next to them. And thank God too, because we need a few babies in this world. I'm only asking you to give me a chance. Men never know the tender secrets of the female body like women. You might come to enjoy it."

Gabby expected this speech. She had heard it before and had managed to defend herself. In a low voice, she whispered, "That's what I'm afraid of. But then you, Lydia, would soon kick me out of your bed to find a new lover. That's your way; I've watched it for years. I'll never judge you for being who you are. But the problem is that I fall in love with those I sleep with. It's always been true for men and I suspect the same would go for a woman. I love you, Lydia, but I won't let you break my heart. This would only get in the way of far more important things we must do together."

"Nothing is forever. Eventually, we'll both wear out our sex organs. You know I won't force myself upon you. When you're ready just take a few steps to my cot."

"I can't stay here."

"You don't know what you're missing."

"Get ready to film in the desert at Ein Arugot. I'll ask Father Sebastian to take you. He can fill you in on what happened there. Take what's left of Warpath to Jerusalem while I'm gone."

"Will we be in communication?"

"Probably not. I must disappear. I don't know where, but I believe the truth about the *Yeshu* Fragment will break soon. Only then can I come out of hiding."

"And go back to Itamar?"

Gabby whispered in a voice devoid of her usual lucidity, "If he still wants me which I don't think he does."

* * * * *

The Ecole's Peugeot was in dire need of a wash, if not the body then certainly the windshield by now thickly crusted with desert dust camouflaging a splintered crack distorting vision. Gabby noticed that Father Sebastian was by nature a nervous driver who was required to lean forward and squint through sunglasses while his plump fingers over-worked the steering wheel. She wanted to suggest he clean the windshield before proceeding farther, but politely restrained the temptation, girding her teeth in anticipation that the priest would weave off the road, or worse.

West Bank Highway 90 snaked north on a tarmac surface paralleling the Dead Sea. Once south of Jericho, the Dominican scholar steered west along Highway 1, but only for a few kilometers before swerving north again on a narrow bituminous road that curved into rocky terrain alongside a dry gully named in medieval times *Wadi Qelt.*

Here Sebastian stopped the car to retrieve from the trunk a portmanteau stuffed with black clothing. Along with clerical vestments appropriate for an extended stay at the Eastern Orthodox monastery of Wadi Qelt came a surprise he had withheld until the last moment. Standing beside the passenger door he announced, "My new friend Rabbi Gabrielle, I carefully chose a place where men searching for you will never think to look. It occurred to me that a monastery home only to monks would be perfect. Oh, on occasionally women visit, but that's just during the day. By sundown they must leave and the outer gate is locked. Who would think of searching for you in a sacred place reserved only for men?"

Gabby glanced down at the portmanteaux Sebastian handed her, saying, "I hope you're not thinking what I am."

Sebastian's lips widened into a mischievous smile. His eyebrows popped above the rims of his spectacles. "The brethren here are a surly bunch who don't talk much among themselves so you won't be expect to converse with them. Visiting clerics often come for quiet and reflection. Maybe a few words are exchanged now and then, but few sustained conversations. I'm told that some visitors remain completely silent."

"They have women's toilets, don't they?" she asked with a quiver in the voice as though she already knew the answer.

"I doubt it," he responded with an enlargement of the playful smile that had remained on his cheeks. "The brethren relieve themselves in public but only when there are no females around. That generally means after sundown. You'll have to choose your times."

"Showers?"

"None that I know of. The boys bathe in an outdoor pool in the courtyard. You can be discreet. I confess that I observed you and your lady friends at the Dead Sea bathing in your birthday suits. Clearly, none of you were modest about God's supreme creation. Naked men shouldn't embarrass you. I told the abbot, Father Sicirious Alexander, by phone you were a young monk needing seclusion for about two weeks. He offered one of three adjacent caves cleaved into the hillside, just outside the main compound. For a modest weekly fee, of course. Legend has it that the monastery was built here because early Christians lived in adjacent caves, beginning sometime in the Fourth Century. Father Alexander reserved a cave with electricity for you so you'll be in the company of ancient and perhaps holy recluses. No running water, however. One of the brethren will deliver a basket of foods each morning, but expect nothing succulent. Just enough to keep you nourished. You're welcome to eat in the refectory with the others—if you manage to convince them you're a man."

Father Sebastian handed her a black cassock. "Dress yourself in this. I've added a wide-brimmed hat to shield your face."

This was not what Gabby was expecting. But she immediately calculated that there were no better alternatives. As long as there was electricity for her computer (and no poisonous snakes, of course) she knew she could manage. Seclusion would be an incentive to finish Lydia's film script on schedule.

Twenty minutes later, Sebastian's Peugeot came to a stop in a postage-stamp parking lot fronting a wooden footbridge. Once he had switched off the ignition her breathing relaxed. He helped manhandle two medium sized suitcases over a short footbridge fording a gully of verdant greenery.

The multistoried Eastern Orthodox monastery was precariously perched on the cliff constructed of sandstone and volcanic basalt. How this unstable structure resisted tumbling into Wadi Qelt below puzzled Gabby. This mystery slipped from her mind as she battled with growing anxiety how a female might blend into a community of monks.

No one met them at the open gate until a priest in a brown woolen cassock and tattered sandals exposing giant toes emerged from a dark corridor into the bright sunlight. An untamed monkish beard threaded with gray dropped along his chest to a thick leather strap securing the garment to his mid-section. Gabby expected to hear a bellowing voice accompanying such an imposing stature, but his voice neared a whisper as he introduced himself: Father Gregory Airinei, Abbot Sicirous Alexander's representative to the monastery's visitors.

The sight of the ever-smiling Dominican friar Sebastian in conversation with this towering and rather dower Orthodox priest struck Gabby as odd. She knew that generally Latin and Orthodox churchmen kept their distance and even where they shared custodianship of the Holy Sites of Christendom, they rarely exchanged more than rudimentary phrases.

Father Gregory was neither friendly nor unfriendly as he led his new guests along a dark cloister circulating cool air and illuminated by a low-wattage light bulbs strung along lava pillars. The Orthodox priest explained the edifice had been rebuilt after Persians sacked the monastery in 614 A.D. Gabby quickly calculated that was more than 1,400 years before. Clearly, the walls and foundations had been reconstructed many times since then. And most likely had threatened to cascade into the wadi below more than once.

A flimsy catwalk led from the rear of the building along the cliff and from there to gravel path leading to a string of four caves. Fathers Gregory and Sebastian manhandled Gabby's suitcases inside the second. A primitive electric switch beside the opening ignited a low wattage electric bulb dangling from the ceiling. A cot, table, and cushion-less chair were the sole furnishings. Gabby was gratified to find an electric outlet near the light switch, sufficient for powering her MacBook Air. No phone, no toilet, and no bathing facilities. All that, Gregory explained, could be obtained in the public places inside the monastery proper. She was welcome to explore at will and make use of the extensive library, known for its collection of rare documents reaching back to the origins of Christianity. For that, he recommended the services of Brother Barthelme, the acting librarian.

After Gregory left them to settle into the new surroundings, Sebastian reminded her that monks were accustomed to hosting reclusive and often eccentric visitors. It was unlikely they would take much notice of her presence. Yet they were a curious bunch who would probably welcome a new face bearing news for the world they had renounced. Sebastian assured her that at Wadi Qelt she was safe from the European thugs searching for her in the Jerusalem area. If he learned anything to the contrary, he promised to inform her immediately.

Her stomach sank when the Latin priest announced that it was time for him to return the Ecole's Peugeot to Bethlehem. Feeling alone and dependent upon her own resources, she experienced an intense uneasiness with the prospect of extended isolation. No one to talk with for a fortnight was certain to test her fortitude. True, she needed quiet time for work, but not total isolation. She noticed Father Sebastian recoil when she stepped close to embrace him in a departing hug. But it was also noticeable that he didn't pull away. Neither mentioned that Father Benoir Matteau, hero to one and enemy to the other, had forged an unlikely bond between them. Even more importantly, they shared knowledge that the Church of Rome and the Government of Israel had publicly lied by declaring the *Yeshu* Fragment a fraud.

Once alone in her new surroundings, she busied herself by setting up a workstation, including a power connection to service her laptop. Her new office was so primitive it took little time to establish. She assured herself that so long as she remained in her new quarters there was little reason to fear the monks of Wadi Qelt. Her first endeavor was to draft a chronology of historic events, followed by a brief narrative outline. Almost all the facts she needed to assemble were indelibly engraved in her memory. It was largely a question of transcribing what she remembered to electronic text.

After sundown, the call of nature forced her to seek a dark crevice in the rocky hillside to relieve herself. But after slipping on loose rocks littering the path it became clear this was no permanent solution. She needed a proper latrine that she speculated would be situated near the refectory. It was, but unfortunately amounted to little more than a sheet-metal urinal attached to the wall of an illuminated cloister. Apparently monks had little motivation to hide what laymen usually regarded as a private function because there was no screening for privacy. In addition there were three door-less stalls a few steps away, each stacked with a pile of cut newspapers as an economic substitute for proper toilet paper.

She had hoped to find the lavatory unoccupied, but discovered a pair of clerics relieving themselves in the adjacent urinal. Gabby modestly dipped her eyes under the broad brim of the hat provided by Father Sebastian. Since most of the holy men went bareheaded, this alone might draw attention. That prospect impelled her to recite an often-recited phrase seeking Divine help. The monks were in no hurry, forcing her to postpone her own needs. When they finally left, she moved immediately into one of the stalls and worked the ill-fitting male britches down past her knees.

Feeling relief for having completed what should have been a simple task she immediately prepared to seek cover in a dark cloister. Her timing couldn't have been worse. A heavy bearded monk suddenly approached, fumbling to un-tuck a white scapula from his tunic. Before dropping his pants to the knees and completing his business he lifted his eyes to catch Gabby scampering from nearby illumination to a dark passageway. At first she believed that she had escaped discovery but a minute later was dismayed to hear heavy footsteps pounding the passageway behind. The silhouette of a large monk appeared momentarily in light from overhanging electric bulbs. There was a sinister almost threatening quality in the wildness of his presence. His footsteps followed her until she eventually exited the monastery's outer door leading to the gravel pathway and her cave. If the monk was still watching he was aided by a near full moon peaking over the mountainside.

The following evening after she assumed the brethren had retreated to their beds, she ventured again to the toilets, this time having selected the most advantageous route. No one appeared to observe her. This was also true when she concluded her business and left the area. She decided to exploit this opportunity by exploring the monastery's library, known among scholars to possess an invaluable collection of ancient scrolls rivaling what was lost a half-century before in the tragic fire at the Monastery of Santa Katrina in the Sinai Wilderness.

The library's location was not obvious. She assumed the weight of books would preclude housing heavy volumes on an upper floor. That propelled her along a series of descending stairs to the ground floor and a row of cellar vaults hewn from the mountainside. There, a series of electric bulbs hung from the ceiling illuminating a corridor that eventually led to the library. Rather than switch on lights, she explored this treasury of historical records behind a flashlight beam.

Leather-bound volumes collecting dust in uneven piles filled the shelves. For lack of space, smaller bound manuscripts had been crudely stuffed into all corners, some on their sides and others stacked into piles that appeared ready to topple over. Two reading tables provided level space but themselves were piled unevenly with surplus volumes waiting permanent homes. She took note of smudged glass cabinets containing scrolls whose contents appeared so old they had never been committed to book form. It took only a passing evaluation to determine the library contained ancient material paralleling the library housed in Jerusalem's Shrine of the Books. But armed with no more than a flashlight there was a limit to what she could examine.

* * * * *

Two nights later Gabby's curiosity drove her back to the library. Her studies of the Talmud written primarily in Aramaic, the lingua franca of the Middle East for the first 300 years before and 300 years after the turn of the Common Era, prepared her to read Aramaic and some of the cognate Syriac texts. But she was at a loss to read the majority of works in Greek.

The variety of subjects compelled her to conclude that however poorly the brethren at Wadi Qelt had organized their collection its age was unquestioned. How old, that she wasn't prepared to estimate, but she was convinced they stretched back many, many centuries, perhaps as far back as the 5th Century A.D.

Trying to get a sense of an Aramaic text in scroll format remained nearly impossible under a flashlight beam. She was struggling to identify a rolled document when her nose first smelled danger nearby. A combination of onions mixed with halitosis. A breath swept over her ear as she twirled around to see the shadowy form of a towering bearded monk in the dimmed shadow behind her.

"Sorry to startle you, Brother," the monk announced in Hebrew. "I noticed light in the library and came to investigate. We're always fearful of fire. Our collection is irreplaceable. You're our new guest staying in the second cave, are you not?"

She brought the flashlight beam to his chest but did not blind him by directing it to his eyes. Rather than speak, she fulfilled a rehearsed signal practiced for just such an occasion, and brought an index finger to her lips indicating that she was unable to speak. Her lips moved but no sounds emerged. The beam moved away to prevent the monk from studying her features.

He seemed to accept her signal, continuing with his own speech. "I'm Father Barthelme Korius, the librarian here. And, Brother, you don't need to read in the dark." With that he stepped over to a wall-mounted switch and illuminated the library with weak light from incandescent bulbs hanging two meters from the timbered ceiling.

Beside Gabby stood an in inordinately tall monk with high cheeks mostly shielded by a heavy black beard. His thicket of facial hair brought to mind the monk eying her at the urinal.

"Brother, we often talk about you over meals," he said. "New company here is always interesting. Most visitors eat and pray with us in the mornings. We welcome them. But you're different. You're a mystery. We know you work long hours on a computer. You never eat with us. We thought you would join us when we heat water to wash in the courtyard, but you don't come for bathing."

Gabby thought about communicating in writing to perpetuate the myth that she suffered from a speech impediment. But for the moment, it became unnecessary as the monk changed the subject. "May I help you find something here? Nobody at Wadi Qelt knows the library as I do. Hardly any brothers come to read. They're poorly educated men who have little interest in books, especially old ones. So, I'm here alone most of the time. These books are my children. And you're obviously interested or you wouldn't come at night."

Gabby wagged her head in a friendly gesture. Yes, she would like his help in identifying early Christian documents in Aramaic or Syriac but didn't know how to communicate this without writing.

Barthelme inclined his head closer to Gabby's chest and as if fearful of being overheard said, "You're different from visitors. You don't seek company. I ask myself who might come here and avoid our community, such as it is?"

She knew this was not a subject she wanted to engage in and, after returning a manuscript to a pile inside a glass cabinet, attempted to turn and head for the library entrance. Barthelme followed to the doorway, but before she could exit placed a heavy fist on her shoulder to deflect her motion. She attempted to break free but a second hand seized her arm and with a display of strength forced her to turn toward him. "If you're searching for something special here, I offer my services. This library is unique. I'm the only one left who knows what's really here. There's no catalogue system; the contents reside only in my mind. I will come to your cave and we can become better acquainted. If you're here for a while, you'll become lonely like me. You'll find the brethren to be decent but quite dull. You'll want the companionship of someone like me. Someone who reads books."

She maintained her silence until he continued, "For some time now I have been watching you carefully. I'm a lonely monk. Living here strains the body. Healthy men like me, unlike the other wounded brethren living here, need physical company. I will come to your cave later." "

Gabby didn't like the direction of the conversation and pivoted on the balls of her feet to flee. Whatever else Father Barthelme had to convey was lost because Gabby made a second determined thrust to distance herself from him. For a moment she thought she smelled bad breath pursuing, but when finally on the gravel pathway headed to the caves was relieved to find herself once again alone.

Barthelme knew where to find her. She would certainly welcome his help in the library but that she knew was not free. The price of befriending a monk with bad breath and suffering from severe loneliness was more than she was prepared to pay.

* * * * *

In the Monastery at Wadi Qelt Gabby learned that she had few alternatives. Now that she knew the monks were aware of her nocturnal visits she scrupulously avoided leaving her hillside cave until after eight bells when the electricity generator shut down for the night. Yet, even at this late hour she imagined monks in the darkened passageways shadowing her movements, unseen eyes ever following her. At times she would double around to catch a glimpse of whoever was stalking her, but without luck. Monks knew every curve and passageway in the cloister; she did not.

Still her nose sniffed what her eyes did not see. A strong whiff of onions lingering in the air often identified Barthelme's presence. Whether this priest was seeking a new friend or perhaps had become suspicious about her gender she could only speculate.

He was nowhere in sight when, after relieving herself one evening, she followed the beam of her flashlight down a series of sandstone stairs to the bathing pool. Since the monks generally washed early in the morning there was little reason to fear meeting one in this pool. Keeping herself clothed in her woolen habit, she descended along concrete steps into the water and at the last moment shed the garment on the rim of the pool whose temperature retained more than a tinge of the day's strong sunlight. After dunking into the water for a thorough soaking, she stood only to soap her body, then dropped down immediately below the surface for a rinse. Water concealed her flesh until it became necessary to leave. Moisture on her skin caused her monk's habit to cling to her body and outline a feminine form. If Father Barthelme was hidden somewhere in the shadows it was possible he might discover her secret.

She avoided the library that night, remaining in her cave. Her muscles craved exercise but without leaving her lodging to jog on the dirt track leading to Wadi Qelt or perhaps walk the monastery's narrow cloisters, there was no place to challenge them. That meant push-ups and sit-ups on a woven straw mat. Not satisfying, but better than nothing. In her mind she marked off the days necessary to complete the script and escape from this horrible place.

Father Barthelme showed up in the cave entrance the following evening. Gone was the noxious odor. His biblical beard had been shampooed and combed; a bone hairpin secured his hair behind the head. He excused his intrusion upon Gabby's privacy as no more than a desire to be helpful. "There are Syriac documents unread for many years, well before I came to Wadi Qelt. They're not part of the regular collection and are stored in a special compartment with other unrecorded texts. I will show you. It is forbidden to remove them from the library, but I can provide space for you to read. No one will bother you there and I'll be the only person to know what you're reading."

Gabby was definitely interested but in a moment of surprise could not figure out how to hide a feminine voice. The only solution was to whisper a response, as though her vocal chords were impaired. "I'm grateful," she said in a soft pitch to disguise her gender. "For the moment I'm occupied with work here but would enjoy looking at these Syriac documents."

Barthelme stepped closer invading that private space she reserved for intimates. She tried to step beyond it, but the priest maintained the identical distance. He announced, "You're a puzzle, my new friend. At first, I couldn't understand why you have avoided the brethren. That is until I saw you leave the bathing pool. It became clear then. I admit that I was angry because you had accepted the hospitality of our Order and broken our rule about women. But shortly afterward, I asked myself how that affected the sacred brethren. In their ignorance they know nothing; their daily routines have never been changed. You remained here in this cave and seduced no one."

Gabby was alarmed yet not surprised. From her first night at Wadi Qelt she had wondered how she might carry this off.

"I will not reveal your secret, Sister," said Barthelme. "To me, you are a fresh breeze blowing over a lonely life."

Gabby's first words spoken in full voice were, "Thank you, sir. It was never my intention to be disrespectful. I needed time and solitude to perform my work. A Latin scholar arranged for me to stay here and until I crossed the bridge over Wadi Qelt I was unaware of your rules about women."

When Barthelme planted his heavy hand upon Gabby's arm she twisted her torso to disengage from it.

The monastic life is really not for me, but I'm trapped here with nowhere to go," he said in a pained voice. "In my life before entering Wadi Qelt I was not celibate. I have a wife somewhere in Syria. And two children I have only seen twice. It is very hard to discipline one's self against the body's urges. Our natures must fight Nature every day. Is that not true, Sister?"

"I'm sorry to learn that Father Barthelme."

"That's why I watched you in the library. I know you have interest in our books. I was hoping to have someone to talk with. It would give me much pleasure to introduce you to our treasures, works that nobody has read in many years, and certainly not during my tenure as librarian. Of course, clerics in the distant past have read them, but they have either passed away or lost interest. Still, these texts have survived. I know only a little Aramaic. Greek is easy, but the Aramaic and cognate Palmyarese from Palmyra is very difficult. I am hoping you might help identify some of the forgotten scrolls."

This was not what Gabby expected. In an awkward moment she replied, "If I can. But understand please that I am not a linguist. I know ancient Aramaic from my studies, but perhaps not the dialect of your documents. Syriac, only when it resembles Aramaic."

"Let us read together," he said with an uplift in tone. "To have someone interested is a blessing. If we talk together I won't be so lonely."

Gabby read into this suggestion that he was seeking more than intellectual companionship. His aloneness was palpable. She introduced a defense mechanism immediately, "Then we'll meet in the library, perhaps tomorrow night after sundown."

For the first time he smiled widely, revealing a mouth of strong but tobacco stained teeth. He reached forward to offer a hand that she accepted with some reluctance. "Tomorrow in the library. Then we'll come back here."

"That will not be necessary. Let's read together in the library. I don't want you to get in trouble by visiting a woman after hours. That can't be good for you or me, don't you agree?"

She led him to the cave entrance and with a firm hand guided him through the opening to the catwalk leading back to the cloisters. "Tomorrow, after sundown I'll come to the library, Father Barthelme."

He dipped his head in a final salutation and headed back toward lights illuminating the monastery.

* * * * *

A text message from Gabby to Father Sebastian Alejandro in Bethlehem went unanswered until the Latin priest got around to checking his messages. He promised to visit Wadi Qelt soon as he could acquire use of the Ecole's Peugeot, which at the moment suffered from a malfunctioning electronic starter—a temperamental device at best—that often fouled when the humidity rose. The vehicle had to be towed to a mechanic in Bethlehem.

Sebastian appeared at the monastery a day later and was escorted by the Abbot's representative, Father Gregory Airinei, to Gabby's cave where he found her editing her final version of the Warpath script. He appeared to enjoy Gabby's welcoming hug by holding her against his chest for an extra few seconds. She offered to share the remains of her breakfast left in a straw basket, but he politely refused, expressing his eagerness to disclose news he had brought from Bethlehem.

His voice was crisp giving the impression that he had rehearsed this speech while driving through the desert. "Last week Israeli police interviewed me at the Ecole. Two men in plain clothes showed official identification then proceeded to inquire of the Ecole's faculty about the European hirelings searching for you. You can imagine how my colleagues cloistered together often run out of things to talk about. Their fertile imaginations had taken over. Stories they made up out of air seemed to entertain but not surprise the Israel policemen. Of course, they asked me about you, but I told them nothing. Especially that I knew you were here at Wadi Qelt."

"Did they say why they were looking for me?"
"I asked, but they were closed mouthed. They wanted to get information, not share it."

"How did the government officers know about these hooligans? In whose employ?"

"Nothing, except that Palestinian police in Jericho detained two Bosnian suspects for entering Israel with false documents. Visa violations are common and can result in stiff fines and deportation. Apparently one of the Bosnians was carrying a firearm, and that would be far more serious."

Gabby cocked her head to acknowledge that this development had reduced but not eliminated her worry. She was relieved to know that if Palestinian police arrested such men they were probably not Zebulon Sonnenberg's minions. But who had sent them remained a mystery. At least now she could return to Jerusalem and possibly restore her relationship with Itamar.

She asked Sebastian. "Is it possible they were churchmen who fear the *Yeshu* Fragment?"

"That's my thinking. There are underground societies in the Christian world. The Church has always been a private club setting its own rules. It's possible these evil men were paid by those far away. Maybe even…" and here he paused before eventually saying, "Maybe from Holy See itself."

"I've thought about that. Hard to believe though Rome knows as much about the *Yeshu* Fragment as we do. The Catholic world can't hide this forever. I've always believed that one of these days Israel and the Vatican will clash over this."

Sebastian nodded his consent. She felt he wanted to add something but years of censoring his thoughts fortified this silence. Her hand on his shoulder substituted for words, followed by a friendly squeeze. "You'll be happy to know that I've finished the first draft of the War-path script. It goes without saying that no writer really completes a manuscript. There's always rewrites and editing. I'm expecting that Lydia Browner will want major changes. She's probably lost patience with me now. I'd like you to deliver this draft to her in Jerusalem immediately. Will you do that for me?"

Sebastian stood as if receiving a high commission. "Certainly. But if you're finished why not deliver it yourself? You can answer Browner's questions on the spot."

"I would. But while here I've had access to the library and there are several manuscripts in ancient Syriac I'd love to review. Since there's no copy machine and I can't take them with me I must make duplicates by hand. I need three days. While Lydia is reading the script I can make good use of this time. Can you to collect me from here Thursday or Friday?"

"If I can reserve the Peugeot. If not, you'll have to wait until I can. Many staff members at the Ecole have need for it. I don't control the waiting list. No further need for remaining incognito?"

"From what you've told me, it appears safe to move about cautiously. That's not to say there's no further danger. My manuscript is explosive. I held nothing back. Every important detail I know about the fragment is in it. As soon its contents become public things will change dramatically. You, I and Warpath are probably going to need new protection. Have your fellow priests at the Ecole clean their handguns. Expect fireworks, but not quite yet."

Sebastian seemed delighted by the prospect and uttered, "Sooner rather than later. I've been battling with Father Benoir's notes for more than a year now. There's no benefit in further delay." He paused to let his eyes lift over his spectacles. "Yes, I think it's time to bring some light to the Church of Rome. Imagine what a lowly friar like me and a scholarly rabbi have done!"

"Good, my friend. When I had brief possession of the fragment, I believed your mentor Benoir wished me dead. His hired goons tried to end my life. But now that he's gone I no longer feel the same way. Both of us had to get used to the idea that Jesus, the Jew and son of Joseph, was never endowed with his prophetic status and had to learn his trade in a school, much like other professionals learn their trades. Jews like me differ with the Church of Rome only where this man's prophetic life led. I have no hesitation saying that he turned out to be a superb spokesman for the God I personally believe in. The god of love for one's fellowman. But his institutional deification centuries later by the Church is something else and not my business."

Sebastian's smile enlarged pudgy cheeks, almost angelic with the pastel hue of a Niccolò di Pietro masterpiece. "In the long run, the direction doesn't really matter. My church will endure no matter. The more we know about this historical Jesus the stronger our faith will be."

Chapter Seven

When alarming statistics from Itamar's confidential report appeared in *Yedioth Ahronoth,* Israel's most read afternoon newspaper, nobody cared who actually leaked the bombshell statistics. Television in both Jerusalem and Ramallah went ballistic.

In a volatile atmosphere, anti-corruption street demonstrations broke out in Ramallah, along with demands that Fatah officials who dominated West Bank politics be prosecuted for the theft of state property. Fatah responded with a diatribe against hypocrisy in Jerusalem and a propaganda program to punish enemy Hamas officials stirring trouble from their distant stronghold in Gaza. There were promises to force the authorities in the Jewish government to prosecute Itamar Arad for maligning Arab honor by inventing false statistics.

For years Itamar had labored to build a professional working relationship between Israeli and Palestinian archeologists. His labors were rewarded when invited by Palestinian scholars to spend his sabbatical year building up an Arab Antiquities Agency to parallel his own agency in Israel. All this perished when the list was published. Once again, in his opinion, Arab corruption diminished Israel-Palestine comity.

"The PM is furious," reported Moshe Rabinzoloff, the Prime Minister's charge d'affaires, to Itamar in a meeting with three Cabinet ministers, all members of the Government Coalition. "He doesn't blame you for the leak but has made some disparaging remarks about your naiveté in thinking an explosive report like this could remain confidential. Nevertheless, he must hold somebody's feet to the fire. And you can guess who that might be. We all acknowledge that you were required to write this report, but all political wisdom would have dictated that you sit on it. Everybody in our trade knows how to kill something with age-old stalling techniques. Given our current climate, you should have slowed this matter from a crawl to an inert status. What were you thinking when you signed off on the report?"

"That its confidentiality would be honored."

"You've been our Director of Antiquities for more than six years. You know as well as I that there's no honor left in government these days."

Jeremiah Klein, a balding supporter of the PM with sun-dried skin that bucketed into waves on his forehead, scowled at Rabinzoloff saying, "There's enough mismanagement around here to cripple the government. So let's cease accusations and design a solution."

"You obviously have something in mind," said Mariam Oz, Minister of Housing, a matronly grandmother who had weathered Israeli politics for more than twelve years in a left-wing party that had survived by means of clever alliances. "Do bless us with your perspicacity, Jeremiah."

That produced a wide, rather insincere smile to reveal a month of teeth in need of an orthodontist. "Not a perfect solution, I'm afraid, but the best of a bad situation is for Itamar to return to Ramallah. And there, use his old network to convey an essential point: whatever has happened to Palestine antiquities is not really the business of the Government of Israel. Of course, seeing and understanding the rich history of Palestine and Israel is important for Israel's archeology. But as far as our politics are concerned, we don't give a rat's fuck…excuse my tongue, Mariam. The Government of Israel intends to overlook how Palestinian politicians enrich themselves; we will move forward to improve relations despite the crooks in Ramallah. And if we must bed down with the devil, so be it."

The proposal was so bizarre the room was filled with an awkward silence. Eventually, Itamar said, "How long do you think I would last in Ramallah with that message?"

"You're a survivor, my friend," said Rabinzoloff. "I'm sure you understand that without a moment of heroism, you're unlikely to remain long as Director of Antiquities. You have many allies in the Government, but sometimes a good head such as yours must fall. You handled the matter of the *Yeshu* Fragment with aplomb. That can't be said for your companion, Dr. Lewyn, who incidentally nobody seems to know her whereabouts."

"The *Yeshu* affair is not over yet," warned Itamar, knowing far more about it than he was prepared to disclose. On this matter the Prime Minister had pushed him into a corner. Now he was pressing him into an even more uncomfortable position.

"And what if I don't return from Ramallah?" he asked.

"I wouldn't fear that," replied Rabinzoloff. "It's our supposition that President Mazoor and his band of felons will like what they hear from you. For them, stealing is nothing but business-as-usual. As long as we continue to tolerate their thievery, they'll be happy to carry on with us. It's their culture, you know. Their people expect nothing less."

In the end, Itamar felt the Cabinet members had led him to the guillotine. They were prepared to whitewash the leak of a confidential report, and at the same time blame him for compiling the list in the first place. Kill the Messenger. Viewing him as the cause of the unpleasantness, they expected him to repair the damage. And if that required facing the unknown in Ramallah, what alternative had he?

* * * * *

Cordial as always, Taalal Nahashibi, senior advisor on the Palestine Council and chief advisor to the President, trumpeted into his cellphone, "Last person in the world I expected to hear from. It is truly Dr. Arad? Since our business together in Istanbul didn't fare well, I was hoping *never* to hear from you. For what have I the pleasure of re-opening that sad affair?"

Itamar released a nervous giggle and, referring to his part in stopping the theft of archeological treasures from Jericho, announced, "That *is* over, sir. The present is too precarious for us to dwell on the past.

"Your report on the state of Palestinian archeology didn't go over well in Ramallah. It was a biased and unfriendly summation. Until emotion subsides, I wouldn't advise that you show your face anywhere in Palestine. As you well know we have too many uncontrollable hotheads here these days. As in Israel, the extremists hold us hostage."

Itamar let that observation sink in for a few moments before addressing the reason for his phone. "Despite finding ourselves on opposite sides in Istanbul, I've always found you to be a reasonable man with the best interests of your country at heart. Because of that

I would like to visit you at a secured place and deliver an important message from the Prime Minister."

"You're timing is terrible. As you well know, our relations with your government go up and down, and I'm afraid that your report has extinguished the few embers of friendship left. The Peace Process is officially in deep freeze."

"That's why we must talk. To demonstrate my sincerity, I'm prepared to accept the personal danger and meet with you anywhere in the Palestine Authority.

"Too damned dangerous. We can't control extremists here any better than you do. Why take the risk?"

"I'll assume that risk. Nobody will know I'm coming except you. Can you suggest somewhere we won't be noticed?"

Taalal thought about that in a long moment of silence before making a decision. "I owe you and Gabrielle Lewyn a favor for letting me off lightly on the Jericho matter. You could have made it far more costly for me. Why you did remains a mystery, yet I possess a good memory and have not forgotten. Let's try the Village of Gaziante where my school friend owns a hillside restaurant. Best baklava in Palestine. I'll send you directions."

"I'm obliged to you, sir," answered Itamar.

"No, Minister. I'm the one obliged to you for dealing kindly with me in Istanbul. Now be careful in the Palestine Authority. If you wish I can arrange the security."

"That won't be necessary. Nobody but you will know I'm coming."

* * * * *

Itamar planned to travel to Gaziante as inconspicuously as possible, entering Palestine by city bus and, once in the village of Al Birah, hiring a taxi for the final ride to Gaziante. There was some confusion in the mind of the taxi driver as to the location of designated restaurant, but after several fruitless circles discovered a small sign and a pathway to the restaurant flowered by multi-colored oleander.

Taalal was not there when Itamar entered a few minutes past 3:00 p.m., when most of the patrons were finishing heavy lunches. A series of ceiling fans circulated a breeze over the indoor dining, though most of the clientele seemed to have preferred the balcony deck with its vista overlooking a neatly sculpted olive-orchard. Disguised in simple

Arab clothing with a baseball cap hiding his features from the sunlight, Itamar ordered a bottle of Taybeh Golden, a Ramallah brew he had become accustomed to drinking during his sabbatical year.

Taalal, who appeared heavier and less well-kept than Itamar remembered, hugged his school friend and chatted amiably with staff near the front cash register. He did not search for Itamar, yet either by instinct or a prearranged signal by the proprietor knew at which table to find him.

Heavy eyelids and deep trenches in the minister's forehead suggested to Itamar the grinding pressures of administering Palestinian affairs. A well-manicured moustache hung over bleached white teeth, a new vanity in Arab culture. He surveyed the clientele in the immediate vicinity of the table before taking Itamar's hand in a professional shake. No sooner had he made himself comfortable, two cups of sweet Turkish coffee arrived, followed by a platter piled with three types of baklava, all liberally dusted with powdered sugar.

Itamar wanted to launch into a speech he had prepared but knew that courtesy demanded he honor the Arab custom of edging into a business matter only obliquely. And that, never until having consumed at least two full cups of coffee.

It was Taalal who opened conversation. "We noticed that my good friend Gabrielle was absent from your press conference regarding the fragment with the name of Jesus. The posting was a total surprise to our Christian community in the Palestine Authority. Then when the fragment suddenly appeared on YouTube, we were skeptical. Of course, the Vatican is not to be trusted in this business. Or, for that matter, your government. Something smells fishy here. We took note that Gabrielle wasn't present at the press conference. I don't expect you endangered your life entering Palestine to monitor Palestinian reaction to this bombshell."

"A complicated matter," Itamar sighed. "I'm afraid I don't know where Gabrielle is. You probably know we've been very close. But the times have estranged us a bit."

Taalal stared at an empty cup of coffee, seemingly lost in thought. Itamar believed he caught the Palestinian minister in a moment of confusion. He followed up, "Any idea where I might find her?"

"Yes, as a matter of fact, I do."

"Where?"

"Now safe in the Palestine Authority. But it wasn't always that way. Some religious men loyal to Fatah told our security people that a band of thugs from Bosnia were looking for her. At first, we thought that your people sent these goons. But a local investigation didn't confirm that."

Taalal's disclosure that Gabby was in the Palestine Authority took Itamar by surprise. "Where is she?"

"As I just said, she's safe."

"Can you tell me more?"

"She's in a sheltered place; that is, if she stays put and doesn't attempt to move around. My people watched the Bosnians, who never seemed to have a clue about her whereabouts. We concluded they were amateurs. There was no reason for us to arrest them because they had done nothing illegal. Our people passed their identities to your security people who, I was told, arrested them on visa violations. As far as I know they're now home in Bosnia."

Relieved to know Gabby was safe, Itamar pursued, "Have you seen her?"

"No. During the affair in Istanbul we became close friends. You know she stayed at my home. But those times are over. I may not be a brilliant minister, but I'm wise enough to know when to leave the past behind. Gabrielle is the kind of woman who could make a man like me lose his senses and get into deep trouble. I'm a married man and an affair between a Palestinian and Jewess wasn't destined for a long future. I've already made my mistakes with Gabrielle and would advise you to do likewise. But you didn't risk coming here to talk about Gabrielle Lewyn, now did you?"

"No. I came to talk about the list of lost artifacts in Palestine. You know it arose out of my employment with the Palestine Council for Culture and Tourism last year. At the time it seemed prudent for me to use the computational skills of my ministry in Jerusalem to develop a comprehensive register of Palestinian archeological treasures. I believed that to be a good start getting control of Palestinian artifacts. As my staff began the project it became obvious that many of these treasures had slipped out of public sight. They existed on paper but not in reality."

A customer who stopped at the table to share his observations on an administrative matter under discussion by the government distracted

Taalal's attention. Itamar was forced to wait until this conversation had run its course and Taalal assured the man that his views would be communicated in Ramallah.

Back to the previous subject, Itamar continued, "When I returned to Jerusalem, as Director of Antiquities, I was required to make a report. This I did, including the gruesome statistics about the open theft of Palestine's artifacts. And this report, because we knew it to be extremely embarrassing to the Authority, was given the highest level of confidentiality. The Government of Israel leaked absolutely nothing to the press. But, as you can imagine, classified material is routinely shared with the entire Cabinet, and here's where the trouble began. You understand our divided government. One or more of the Cabinet Ministers, most probably those unfriendly to the Palestine Authority and our joint Peace Process leaked the report. No doubt a minister from the settlements. Please be aware that this was not the work of the Prime Minister, who you must take my word, was personally both appalled and furious. That man has a temper. And he was burning hot, some of his heat directed at me. I have been authorized by him to extend our apologies, and most importantly, to tell your government that the report will have no bearing on my government's relations with the PA. What has occurred with your antiquities is your business, not ours. Nothing, from our point of view, has changed. We cannot undo the embarrassment caused. We can only continue as if the report never happened."

Taalal said nothing when Itamar finally finished his soliloquy. He simply wagged his head, until finally saying in a saddened voice, "Israel has made our position very difficult; but ultimately, we must share the blame. As a mere minister in the Authority, I cannot accept your apology; but as someone with dirty hands in this business, I personally assume a measure of responsibility. That I took nothing for myself from the Jericho treasures is now a matter of record. One hundred percent of the funds received from sale of Jericho artifacts went to pay for the Palestinian land deeds we purchased from the Turks. For us, the operation turned out to be a colossal waste of money. When your agents destroyed the Turkish Recordation books, they destroyed our hopes to reclaim Palestine property through your courts. I must compliment myself on an excellent plan, however useless it proved to be."

Itamar appreciated Taalal's rather shrewd, patriotic role in the affair. For that reason he maintained confidence in the Arab's integrity. A slight tilt of his head assured Taalal he concurred with his evaluation.

The Palestine minister said, "You've made life difficult for Palestinian officials. I don't expect any to forgive you or the government. Hard feelings take time to heal. But we've both been around long enough to understand that in time the passion of the moment subsides. And at some point we'll return to normal, whatever such a normal may be."

"Thank you, sir. I will report to my government that the apology has been rendered, but not accepted. You're right. Only time can heal this wound. "

"Take care returning to Jerusalem. And I promise to let you know if matters change with Gabrielle. But for now, be assured she's okay."

* * * * *

Itamar requested a meeting with Porcupine by secured email and, as expected, there was no immediate reply. He knew the intelligence agent to be unsocial yet not one to avoid reading his email. A second email brought a terse response.

What do you wish to talk about?
I'd like to do this face to face. I'm buying lunch or dinner whichever you prefer.
I know what's on your mind and can't talk about it.
Indulge me. I know you have no one at home to cook dinner for you.
So tonight at Ayellet on King George Road. 8 p.m.

Porcupine was there before 8:00, seated exactly where Itamar imagined he might be, in a banquette against the back wall with a full view of diners as they entered the restaurant. As Itamar approached, his eyes rose from the screen of an I-Phone. The Director of Antiquities slipped into a chair facing the intelligence agent. Both men expected the other to open conversation.

After an extended silence, Porcupine said, "Nothing. You don't have to be genius in the spy business to know we don't communicate directly with our people in the field. And in Syria these days, never. Too damn dangerous for people willing to do this kind of work.

Despite common miscomprehensions, we have more than ice water in our veins."

"You know I'm worried about Kar'ine."

"That's obvious. I know a lot about people but could never understand their romantic sensibilities. She's a commendable woman, I'll grant you that. But why a man of your intelligence and with a partner like Gabrielle Lewyn—what is it about this Syrian chick that grabs you? She's exotic as hell, gorgeous to look at but forbidden fruit. She's no reason for you to go off the deep end."

Porcupine's analysis annoyed Itamar. However much he needed his help, he didn't believe he possessed the capacity to understand his internal conflict. Yes, of course, he valued and loved Gabby. Deep down, he believed that the spat with her would calm. Eventually, the *Yeshu* matter would resolve itself and when it did, their differences would disappear into history. But Kar'ine was another matter. She had slipped into his life obliquely and there remained a part of a complex emotional life he had become accustomed to. In some ways he felt responsible to help fix a life broken by a bad marriage and a civil war filled with horror. In others, he empathized with her solitude. Without children, home or county, she survived only by her wits. And he could not get out of his mind the evening in Istanbul they spent together in bed. Gabby had always been a lusty, sharing sex partner, but Kar'ine was a wild feline that elicited from him unknown passion. She had told him in no uncertain terms that they would never duplicate that wonderful night consumed in each other's bodies. A foolish man might dream she would change her mind. That, he knew the strong-willed Kar'ine would never do. What she had shared with him about her sex life in Damascus was as intimate as a woman could be. He cherished that forthright intimacy. Even if they never made love again, he still wanted her in his life.

For a brief moment Porcupine seemed to exhibit a modicum of compassion for Itamar's conflicted feelings, saying, "Just so there's no misunderstanding, friend, there's been absolutely no contact with her in Syria. And we intend to keep it that way. But as of this moment, we're pretty sure she's alive and functioning."

Itamar's concentration suddenly perked. "Now how would you know that?"

"I'm telling you this only because you're a fellow government servant. What you're about to hear is highly confidential and meant to stay that way. Understood?"

Itamar responded, "Of course."

"Her trading is done through a private bank in Beirut. We know how many American dollars goes into that account, and it's a matter of simple arithmetic to monitor daily how many are removed. Only Kar'ine and a trustee in the States know the passwords for removing funds. So if money is leaving the account on a reasonable schedule, we can assume she's operating as planned. If the withdrawals stop we'll know there's trouble."

"You've got a plan to get her out?"

Porcupine manufactured an artificial Hollywood stage smile and declared, "Why of course we do. But I must confess to you as a fellow government official, our plan isn't worth shit. We're counting on Kar'ine's judgment when to run. If she's smart she'll grab her winnings from the table and skedaddle."

Itamar accepted a wine list from a middle-aged Russian Jewish waiter who irritated him with an overly theatrical recitation of the evening's specialties. Two menus followed.

"How's Gabrielle these days?" Porcupine asked.

Itamar's eyes bounced from the edge of a large maroon menu, replying, "Gabb and I had a falling out. But she's a social animal who picks up friends everywhere. As far as I know she's holed up in the Palestine Authority somewhere. If you or your friends know where, I'd be grateful to learn. It's time for us to make up."

"Sorry. That's not our terrain."

* * * * *

Gabby lived on tenterhooks, fearing that Father Barthelme would break his pledge and share his discovery with the brethren. But he didn't. In fact, during the evenings when the cloister emptied and monks retired to an even quieter existence in their beds, he stayed awake shuffling around in the library, constantly hovering over Gabby. Though it was forbidden to have food or beverages near this timeless literary collection, tea from the refectory materialized along with brown-sugar cakes never delivered to her cave during the morning food distribution.

It was the historian in Father Barthelme who explained how the location of the Monastery at Wadi Quid served medieval Roman and Byzantium merchants plying trade routes east and west along the famed Silk Road. And as early Christians immigrated from the West to the eastern frontiers of the Holy Roman Empire, they established a series of trading colonies complete with sanctuaries and storehouses joining Jerusalem and Palmyra. Over the centuries Orthodox churches replaced village sanctuaries and permanent villages, the temporary trading markets. When devout holy men could no longer suffer these over-crowded and crime-ridden cities, they built remote monasteries, such as Wadi Qelt.

Barthelme produced a frayed, dog-eared dictionary in the original semi-cursive Aramaic script. As a student of the Talmud Gabby could read it. Though the syntax and vocabulary of the Aramaic language had evolved over the years, the script in which it was originally written had remained largely unchanged for two millennia. And that proved true for copies of church records originating in Palmyra sometime in the 5th Century A.D. Father Barthelme spoke of an Aramaic sub-dialect in Palmyra that church scholars referred to as Palmyrese.

Gabby noticed that each night the Orthodox priest narrowed the distance to her on the workbench they shared alongside a wooden refectory style table. He usually arrived in the library before her, his beard freshly shampooed and the food stains in his cassock laundered away. Tobacco breath replaced halitosis that in the past seemed to hang in the air around his presence. She knew him to be a dedicated smoker of odiferous cigars but in the confines of the library he refrained.

She sensed it was only a matter of time before this priest's apparent needs for company would translate into confrontation. This meant accelerating the transcription of documents she intended to study later in Jerusalem. Timing was not in her favor, for just as she was preparing to leave Wadi Qelt Barthelme introduced her to a forsaken cabinet of parchment scrolls long since overlooked by Church scholars.

That piqued Gabby's curiosity. "What kind of documents?"

"Letters. Filled with theological questions that early Christians in Palmyra asked of Church authorities in Jerusalem. We know these early Eastern Christians had little schooling and relied heavily upon Christian scholars in the West. Syrian Christians deferred theological questions to Church Fathers in the Holy Land. I've read that sometimes these inquiries are called *Responsa*."

Upon an initial inspection, Gabby identified copies of documents dating back to the late 5th Century A.D. from archives that miraculously survived in the ruins of the Trumanin Basilica. Barthleme commented. "Somehow, I know not how, these manuscripts were brought from Palmyra to Wadi Qelt. Maybe for safety."

Gabby cobbled together four letters of interest hoping to finish copies before she left the monastery. Unfortunately, the monks there had no need for a copy machine and therefore none existed. She considered making copies by hand in the library, but that was impractical with Barthelme hovering nearby and continuously cramping her workspace, his shoulders rubbing hers and occasionally his hand grasping hers to point out a phrase of significance.

Each night before midnight he usually trailed behind her in the cloistered passageways, each night approaching closer to her cave entrance, perhaps awaiting an invitation to go inside. She took note of his yearning for physical contact in minute movements of his lips and when he came near, a film of sweat. Never a fan of clerical celibacy in the Church, she attempted to understand this strange man to whom she was indebted. But as time progressed she sensed that his sexual discipline could no longer be trusted. Once he managed to trap her inside the cave her avenue for escape would be blocked. She knew herself to be athletically fit, but unable to resist such a powerful man, especially one driven by years of unnatural abstinence. Barthelme, certainly not an ignorant man, must have assumed that her presence in the monastery would end abruptly. Time was not on his side.

With the clock ticking for her as well, Gabby felt pressure to transcribe four Responsa letters not in the library but in her private dwelling during daylight hours. To do so required secretly removing three manuscripts that she intended to return to their proper place later. That required distracting Barthleme, then slipping these documents inside her cassock. No easy task because despite years of monastic life pouring over minute texts, the priest wore no spectacles and exhibited no signs of diminished eyesight. Even small and faded script he read easily. His hawkish eyes were constantly upon her.

One evening Gabby excused herself to make an emergency trip to the urinal. She returned with her cassock partially unbuttoned. In a moment when Barthleme's eyes were anchored over a Greek text, she stuffed three scrolls through the folds of the garment and out of the monk's sight. Back in her quarters, she dedicated herself to transcription during daylight hours when she felt assured Barthleme was occupied with communal duties. But after dark, matters were different. And with no lock on the flimsy entrance cave door, her sleep was uneasy.

She managed to transcribe a complete Turmanin letter and return it successfully to the library. Her plan was to work on the second scroll the following morning and return the document that evening. If successful, the third would follow the next day.

On her cot a combination of fear and uncertainty disturbed her sleep. Sometime after one in the morning she finally fell asleep but was awakened by the weight of a thick winter blanket covering her torso. As she stirred from sleep to awareness, she became conscious of human body over hers. A familiar grunt along with a whiff of tobacco breath identified her attacker. A second later a large hand pawed at her breast. With a herculean thrust she attempted to free herself, but the attacker re-distributed his weight to keep her pinned down. Next, she tried rotating underneath to free herself but was restrained by a combination of the cot's wooden frame on one side and a strong thigh on the other. The mass above crushed her chest collapsing the lungs. She understood in that flash moment how rapists subdued their prey by depriving them of air. Fighting to breathe there was no resistance. Barthleme's second arm covered her mouth as she gagged on a dry scream that went nowhere in the desert cave.

With his free hand he groped at cotton underpants she customarily wore for sleeping. They protected her private parts only long enough for fingers to bypass the formality of tugging her garment below the thigh. Instead they ripped downward until the cotton gave way exposing her groin. In the struggle she managed to replenish a half-lung of lost air, and this provided a spurt of energy to renew resistance. Fingernails and teeth became cutting weapons, wildly scratching and biting anything within range. She squirmed and rolled in the confined space determined to protect her privates from an erect penis she felt probing between her legs. This enormous man was nimble as he was dominating, shutting down each of Gabby's defensive maneuvers one by one.

Despite her continuous flailing, he managed to direct his organ between her legs until it found an opening. A surge of pain shot through Gabby, but it was short-lived. Father Barthelme discharged himself almost immediately after penetration. The rape was brutal, fast and surgical. The moment he withdrew his body her lungs refilled with life-giving oxygen. Breathing heavily, she howled, "You goddamned sonavabitch! Father Airinei will cast you into the desert for the jackals to chew."

Barthelme partially sat up to straighten his own cassock and released an artificial laugh. "I think not. If you mention a word, I will tell how you stole manuscripts from our library. My superior will bring charges of theft to the Palestine police. And that will come after my clerical brethren have punished you privately for other offenses in Wadi Qelt."

In the course of her rabbinical life, Gabby had counseled several raped women. Always a matter of remote empathy. How could a woman feel for another until she herself had been violated? Gabby wanted to cry, but that satisfaction she would not provide Father Barthelme. In the moment of sorrow for herself, the priest's semen trickled along her thigh. Thank God, she advised herself, it was not time in her cycle for pregnancy. She knew that from this moment on she would be a wounded soul, perhaps mistrusting her own body, as raped women often testified. Still, she knew that in one way she might be different. However horrible the experience, suffering was not inevitable.

The night's horror convinced her that come the morning sun, she would leave Wadi Qelt, whether or not Father Sebastian showed up to whisk her home in the Peugeot.

Instead of flouting his success, Father Barthelme rose from the cot and barely straightened his back. His dark eyes no longer ravished the feminine beauty he had dominated. Gabby's rage abetted long enough to notice how the man appeared broken, with eyes that refused to meet hers.

"I am taking back what you have stolen from the library," he said in a low voice while shuffling to her desk and removing the second scroll she was working on.

"I stole nothing. I intended only to transcribe the text for reading later. It would have been returned undamaged."

"God will judge you," the Orthodox priest growled, stepping to the cave entrance.

"And you too, Barthelme. Mine was a fault of judgment; yours an eternal and unpardonable sin against women."

The priest was in no mood to debate. He stepped through the door into the night, leaving only heavy footsteps behind.

The silence fitted Gabby's gloom. Feeling alone and abandoned, she sobbed with a wail that originated near her abdomen and resounded off the narrow walls of the cave. No effort was made to restrain her tears. Time passed without measure. Eventually, she regained her senses, bringing her powers of reason to what had occurred. That self-pity should take command of her emotions offended the internal strength she aspired to. Weeping was intense, but short-lived. Dropping back to her cot to figure out her next move, her thoughts were disturbed by liquid from Barthelme dripping along her inner leg. It was essential, she thought, to bathe, but that would require entering the cloister. Suddenly the precautions against being identified as a woman became unimportant. After what she had experienced, the secrecy of her gender no longer mattered. Bathing was essential, even if it risked unmasking her womanhood. In an undefined way, she welcomed it.

The catastrophe of the night was slightly mollified by the absence of monks near the bathing pond. She was able to strip in tepid water left from the morning bath and introduce soapsuds into the internal cavity between her legs. Over and over she rinsed, then re-soaped, with each repetition destroying the priest's seminal cells and a small measure of his bitter memory.

The hardest task occurred after retreating to her cave. There, ensconced in her monastery blanket, she peered into the darkness and wrestled with a path forward. It was possible to become embittered, but that she knew from past experience was self-punishing. To seek justice from the Orthodox monks at Wadi Qelt seemed even more futile. Members of a tight club of clerics together suffering from self-imposed isolation, they would never feel the pain of a female who had accepted their hospitality under somewhat false pretenses.

In the end, Gabby was driven to an unwanted resolution. Not only was it necessary to acknowledge the rape, but she had no alternative but to relegate it to an unpleasant past experience and then silently, begrudgingly walk away. To erase this sordid event from her mind would require super-human strength, strength she believed capable of producing. She kept repeating to herself a mantra that there was nothing sacred in a vagina designed for removing bodily wastes and occasionally doing double service for childbirth. Her rape had permanently destroyed neither of these functions. The damage caused by Father Barthelme was entirely in her mind, and that, she pledged was subject to her will.

As for sharing this ugly event with others in Jerusalem, her first thought was that it would serve no purpose. Since it occurred in the remote desert, unseen by any but the rapist himself, there was no way others would ever learn of it. If she willed it, no one on the planet would ever know.

The only bright light was that in his loss of control, Father Barthelme had apparently overlooked the third parchment scroll awaiting transcription on a small shelf. It had always been in her plan to return everything after transcription. But seeing that she would depart Wadi Qelt at sunrise, there was no time remaining. Since Father Barthelme had never catalogued this ancient collection, no one would ever notice the loss of a single document. Were it to be returned to the monastery's library it might remain lost in a remote cabinet for a century or two before new scholars got around to deciphering it. Even if Barthelme eventually discovered the missing scroll, it was unlikely he would draw attention to his role in its loss.

In Gabby's mind the matter had been decided, for right or wrong, before sunrise when she crossed the wooden bridge fording Wadi Qelt en route home to Jerusalem. She took with her one suitcase; the second remained in the cave. On the dirt road leading west, she joined a Bedouin shepherd herding eight goats. About six kilometers from the monastery, she received a call on her cell phone from Father Sebastian. He was just leaving Bethlehem in the Ecole's car and if she walked in the same direction he could meet her in a little more than an hour.

While walking to rendezvous with Sebastian it occurred to her that she had failed to mention being raped. That was a good sign; she had passed the first hurdle.

* * * * *

In Jerusalem Gabby caught up with Lydia Browner near the swimming pool at the King David Hotel. She was standing among a cluster of athletic men in a black bikini that contrasted with her golden hair pulled back and fastened into a ponytail by a black bow. Her figure throughout all their years of friendship had remained only a smidgen less than perfect hourglass. Animated in conversation with the menfolk, obviously taken by her beauty, she failed to notice Gabby's approach. For an extended moment, Gabby stood in silence, wrestling with what she expected to be a cool reception. Father Sebastian had delivered her manuscript four days before, plenty of time for Lydia to review it. Since they enjoyed a long history of disagreements she anticipated a hostile reaction.

But it didn't come. In fact, when Lydia finally noticed Gabby standing in silence, she rudely abandoned the solicitous males and stepped forward to envelop her in an affectionate bear hug. She brushed Gabby's cheek with her own and broke off with a sisterly kiss. "God, I'm glad to see you," she exclaimed. "Where the hell were you? I tried to find out but nobody knew. Absolutely nobody."

"Father Sebastian delivered the script to you?" Gabby asked as they searched arm in arm for a place to talk. It turned out to be a table recently vacated by a heavy-set, mustachioed male with sun-dried wrinkled skin and an equally heavy female companion wearing a Panama cane hat. "Of course. It's wonderful, Gabb. I can't believe you never actually wrote a film script before."

"You like it?" Gabby voiced her surprise.

"Love it, but there's one tremendous problem, my love, and it's a major, major flaw."

Gabby inhaled for what she expected to be a Gatling gun fusillade.

"It's actually far too good for me and Warpath. We're a small mom-and-pop shop. I'm aggressive and competent, but it's all-wrong for Warpath. Incidentally, I had to release Claire and Gila. There's only you and me now. Nobody left at Warpath to do this script justice. To do it right will cost bundles of money, professional promotion and, yes, star actors. Gabb, you haven't written a documentary script but a movie narrative. You know the subject is big, very big. It's fresh and enlightening, and it touches the core of Christianity."

"Are you thinking Hollywood?" Gabby interrupted.

"That's exactly what I'm thinking. Only that means much more time, and far more money, and dealing with California assholes along with stupid, avaricious producers. But it's worth it, friend. Everything

I've learn in this trade tells me we have a winner here, something much bigger than both of us ever imagined."

"Well…,"Gabby swallowed saliva accumulating in her throat. "I haven't thought in such terms… Have you made inquiries with associates in Southern California?"

"No. I couldn't do that without first talking with you. I made a pledge not to reveal anything about the *Yeshu* Fragment. One word from me in Hollywood and your secret will skip around the world faster than World Cup soccer scores. The subject is explosive. There's no way to keep it under wraps once conversations begin."

Gabby nodded. That much she had already acknowledged to herself. It was only a matter of time before the truth became public and, once it did, her role in events surrounding it would be obvious. It hadn't been forgotten that somebody had put a bounty on her head. As soon as everybody learned of the fragment she might become a new target. She had hoped that whoever had posted the YouTube photo would come forward. But that had never occurred and she had come to believe it wouldn't. Which left the Israeli Prime Minister and Itamar, and they had no reason to pursue the truth. No matter what the consequence, she alone could bring light to two thousand years of darkness. And what better way than with a Hollywood extravaganza?

* * * * *

Gabby was reticent but nevertheless eager to reunite with Itamar. She had long been aware that after Istanbul he was not the same man she once knew. Something had happened in Turkey when on assignment for the Israel government, something he either couldn't or wouldn't share with her. Such secrecy she had come to accept as essential to his government job. That she could live with, but something more personal lurked in this matter, most probably another woman. And as she mentally rehearsed her search for him in Istanbul, she concluded it was the antiquities dealer she had met briefly in the Istanbul shop of Korkut Murat. She recalled a very beautiful Muslim woman capable of attracting most red-blooded males, even Jewish males often enchanted by Gentile women. As far as Gabby was aware this woman remained in Turkey after Itamar returned to Jerusalem. Still, the tail of whatever had happened there continued to wag the present.

There was still another agenda on Gabby's mind. Once home in Jerusalem she confirmed her decision not to mention the rape at Wadi Qelt. Other than her gynecologist no one needed to know. She recognized pathology in this decision; still it was consistent with her pragmatic outlook. No matter how empathetic Itamar might be, and she knew him to be a kind but not a gushingly empathetic person, no man wanted to know that his bed-partner had been violated by another man. To share details was certain to affect their love making, if and when she succeeded in re-coupling with him.

For the moment her decision to go public with what she knew about the *Yeshu* Fragment eclipsed the bitter memory of rape. That disclosure she didn't want Itamar to learn from Jerusalem's fertile rumor mill, or even worse, from the Israeli press. The sooner she shared with him the existence of Father Benoir's notes and her film script the better. Bringing Itamar up to date was an essential first step toward bridging their separation.

But the man she found in their Jerusalem home was even less open than the one with whom she had bitterly fought with over making the photocopy. Itamar, always a gentleman even under adverse circumstances, immediately accepted her return home, but lacked enthusiasm or passion. She nevertheless harbored hopes (perhaps unrealistic) of cleansing the memory of rape by having sex with the man she loved. But their first night in bed they kissed goodnight like familiar school chums rather than lovers, neither initiating intimacy.

The next morning she planned to tell him about publishing Father Benoir's notes and more importantly to convert her documentary script into a Hollywood film. Since Itamar had failed to stock breakfast foods in their kitchen, they visited *Ayelet ha-Shakar* neighborhood café for coffee and breakfast muffins. He took the opportunity to introduce a subject on the top of his mind, saying, "I'm seriously considering resigning from the Agency. Haven't pulled the trigger yet, but I'm almost ready."

That took her by surprise. "Iti, you love your work and I can't think of anyone doing it better. Where would the government get another honest man like you? A corrupt successor will use the post as a cash cow. Your predecessor enriched himself and ended in prison."

"I can hardly do my job these days," he said in a voice charged with emotional exhaustion. "Our noble politicians look at me as their hired gun to keep them in office. The press leak about my register of stolen Palestinian artifacts has been a nightmare. *You-know-who* clandestinely sent me to Ramallah to apologize to the Palestinian crooks for revealing their thievery. These days nobody in the government gives a shit about the truth. Cabinet members said publicly that I injured Israel's best friends in the Palestine Authority. What friends? What injury? What hurts is that I did no more than compiled the report; self-righteous Cabinet members leaked it to the international press. Now they want to cashier the messenger."

"*Mumzerim*, Bastards. But that's got to blow over."

"Sure, everything blows over in time; I might be dead when it finally does."

"You won't do anything drastic, will you, Iti?"

He took a long sip from a coffee mug that had been delivered to their table, along with four fruit-filled pastries painted with an egg glaze. The liquid remained in his mouth before he let it drop into the throat. "You know me, Gabb; that's not my style. I brew slowly, not erupt. Too many important things on my desk to complete before I accept a university job and settle into complete boredom."

When assured that Itamar had said everything he wanted on the subject of his employment, Gabby elected to introduce what was on her mind. "You still angry with me about making a photocopy of the fragment?" she asked.

"I was pretty hot, but I later reckoned that it was only a matter of time before whoever had posted it on YouTube would strike again. When that happens, we'll all have egg on our faces. Since the leaker hasn't struck again, it's time to be proactive. I never believed, like Zebulon Sonnenberg, that you were the leaker. But before you publish anything, give the old man the courtesy of a *heads-up*. He's always been suspicious of you, you know. Even if he doesn't arrest you he's got the power to make your life miserable. Even if he knows you're innocent his conscience won't be disturbed."

"He's too cunning to throw me into jail. That would only complicate his relations with Rome."

Itamar had already thought that through and concurred. But the P.M. might force her resignation from Shrine of the Book and possibly take steps to destroy her academic career.

That evening at home over a frozen chicken dinner, she told him about the ancient caves at Wadi Qelt. Careful not to mention the rape, she related how Father Barthelme had helped her in the monastery library, and how she had absconded a small Palmyrene document written in Aramaic script. Itamar was far from enthusiastic about this and recommended that she immediately return it to Wadi Qelt.

"Perhaps," she demurred, "but not until after I learn to read it. The language isn't easy for one trained only in Talmud. Palmyrene hasn't been used since Palmyra was sacked in the Fifteenth Century."

"You're aware, I hope, that all foreign antiquities in this country come under my jurisdiction. I'll have to open an investigation and take punitive action upon the investigators' recommendation."

"How long does that take?" she responded, estimating how much time she might need to decipher the document.

For the first time in their conversation, he smiled. "That depends upon *my* discretion. The faster you work the safer you'll be. To cover your beautiful little ass, work off copies and deposit the original with my Authority. We'll lock it up safely until you're ready to return it to Wadi Qelt."

"It wasn't easy to get," she replied.

"In antiquities law, that's as important as a horse tick. Create and sign a note about how you came to possess it. We'll store this note with the original in our safe. If anything happens we don't want anyone believing you stole it for personal wealth."

* * * * *

The partial publication of Father Benoir Matteau's notes in *Biblical Archeology Annals* edited by Father Sebastian ignited a wildfire of speculation. This was the first revelation that a major breakthrough in early Christian historiography had occurred. The article was written in scholarly format with footnotes amplifying Benoir's history of the *Yeshu* Fragment. Overnight, Sebastian became a celebrity first on Israel Television Two, and soon after on interviews for British, French and American news programs. Journalists from around the world jumped on a story that possessed elements of drama, personality, biblical history and mostly, intense conflict with two thousand years of Church doctrine.

"My position at the Ecole in Bethlehem has been terminated," Sebastian told Gabby in her Jerusalem home. "My desk has been removed, along with all my papers. Thank God I took your advice and put the important notes in the Cloud. I think they've even taken my bed."

"That's horrible. You've given your life to the Ecole and made a major contribution. The entire faculty of scholars interested in the First Century knows who you are and what you've accomplished. We won't take this sitting down. Don't worry, for the time being you have a place to stay here with Itamar and me, and an office to work in. Whatever was taken from Bethlehem, we'll replace in Jerusalem."

"My reputation? My work? My pension? My future? It's possible I'll be excommunicated from the Church I've served and cherished all my life."

Gabby had come to enjoy hugging the chubby priest and, what she believed to be more important, because he was a man of God, his flesh touching hers brought a measure of cleansing. The holiness in this Latin priest caused her to wonder about the cause of the Ortho-dox priest's dishonor. Was it loneliness? Unnatural celibacy? Or simple isolation?

To Sebastian she continued, "The world always needs a good scholar. It's possible Itamar and I can find a post for you in Israel. I hope it will never come to that."

"I helped hide you, friend," Sebastian said. "It may happen that now I'll need you to hide me. My supervisors at the Ecole knew all along I was working on Benoir's memoirs. But I doubt they'll now oppose the Church of Rome and protect me."

"Did they ask about Father Benoir?"

"Not really. They revered him while alive, but memory is short. As soon as he was gone, their reverence shifted. So they seldom asked me about Benoir's notes. I didn't want to stir a hornet's nest so I never advertise my work. Now that Benoir is exposed, both for good and bad, they want nothing to do with me."

"Messengers are always the easiest targets," Gabby intoned, her thoughts rushing forward to understand where this was all going.

Gabby and Itamar made ready the guest bedroom for Sebastian and pointed out the hallway hook where keys to their cars hung. Meals would be with them, either cooked by the Itamar-Gabrielle team or in local restaurants. They learned almost immediately that Father Sebastian was seldom at home. In a short time, the subject of Benoir's escapades escalated him into media stardom, including a visit by two Vatican officials sent to escort him to Rome.

Chapter Eight

After closing down the last vestiges of Warpath Enterprises, Lydia traveled from Jerusalem to Los Angeles along with Gabby's documentary script.

She displayed a rare characteristic. Most males and females tend to blot ex-lovers from their lives. Not Lydia. Though she had toned down her sexual appetite, concentrating of late on females, she remained friends with an extensive string of ex-male and female lovers, almost all jealously guarded in her contact list. Whenever possible, she updated old friendships, sometimes in bed, but more often not. Marriage was never an impediment, and sometimes included new spouses.

In the Marriott Residence Inn on South Beverly Drive in Beverly Hills, she phoned Tony Canales, an ex-lover and off-and-on business associate who, after having written four good novels and barely earned enough to cover expenses, reinvented himself as a celebrity literary agent in the firm of Canales, Klugmeir and Morton Literary Agency, in which he was the last surviving partner in the trade.

Lydia had sent ahead Gabby's script, and when she met him for lunch Tony had already read through it, or as he responded, "I inhaled it. If I can't sell this baby I should retire to something less taxing, say dentistry. By the way, do you own the script or Gabrielle Lewyn? And the intellectual property with respect to this Jesus Fragment?"

"We're like sisters. Not lovers, at least not yet though I'm still trying to seduce her. I suppose she possesses the legal rights, but she trusts my judgment. She's deputized me to handle the business points of our venture. I've never seen Gabby reach for a dollar. She has long since stopped practicing as a rabbi, but the spirit of God is in her soul. She wants the world to know the importance of what her deceased boyfriend Tim Matternly discovered at Qumran. She's written the script from personal involvement, fortified by the notes of the deceased Dominican priest, Benoir Matteau."

"Am I to pitch this as historical truth or a *"what-if"* narrative?"

"I'll fire you on the spot if you don't sell this as historical truth. If the industry treats it as fiction or half-truth it's guaranteed to flop. People have been speculating about Jesus from the 1st Century. The Church in Rome has traded in the shadows of mythology. This gives us ammunition to destroy a tired myth and shed light on what really happened at the beginning of Christian history"

"I take it the Vatican has possession of the original Jesus Fragment."

"Why is that important?"

"Because we'll need good attorneys. We don't want the Church to slow us down in legal challenges. That's very expensive and extremely time consuming. A revolutionary work like this can get boxed up in the courts. It will take the wind out of our sails. After reading the script, I'm still not clear. Who posted the Jesus Fragment on YouTube?"

Lydia opened her palms while shaking her head. "Nobody knows. Or if they do, nobody is talking. It remains a mystery. But my guess is once everybody knows a major film is under production and once Father Sebastian's notes are published, shit will hit the fan. Many more people will be asking that question."

Lydia retired to the Marriott in order to let Tony make preliminary inquiries. He explained a well-established process of the trade, beginning with casual phone conversations. Movie producers were inundated with ideas and scripts of all varieties, and in order to spare themselves the toil of weeding through vast piles of scripts and ideas they relied upon favored agents. While it was rare for them to take a phone call from an unknown agent, they were always accessible to Hollywood's movers-and-shakers.

Tony had worked in the industry's trenches for two decades before achieving a respected status. A producer normally returned his calls within 24-hours. They loved one word he used sparingly: "Blockbuster." It was enough to get an immediate interview since the producer knew any genuine blockbuster would be auctioned, not sold directly.

While Tony phoned Lydia each day with an update, they did not meet for another week, during which time he engaged in back-to-back conferences, usually at four or five star restaurants, and always at a secluded table or booth.

Tony had always been enamored by Lydia's beauty. While he was thoroughly aware of her sexual proclivities, that was of little concern to one who understood how she was incapable of sustaining a relationship, and certainly not marriage. But an erotic affair was never to be overlooked, especially if it was concurrent with what promised to be the biggest financial deal of his career.

He suggested they meet for a barefoot walk on the San Monica beach where he might admire Lydia's athletic legs, sculpted ankles and straight toes unbent by high heal shoes. Forecasts called for scattered clouds and stiff winds, Lydia's favorite weather. They rendezvoused on the sand opposite Ocean Park Boulevard.

As Tony had hoped she was attired in tight navy blue shorts and sandals, perfect for trekking in the sand at surf's edge. He came in cargo shorts and canvas shoes also light for carrying as they strolled. Lydia immediately grabbed his arm and clung close to him, an enduring physical closeness he enjoyed while knowing from past experience that she showered this physical affection on all her friends.

"Well?" she could hardly contain her impatience to learn about the reception of Gabby's script.

He put an arm around her shoulder thinking that she had lost none of her youthful muscle tone. That distinguished her from many of his female movie star dates, who he found rather unimpressive without makeup and costume props. "Lots of enthusiasm," he reported. "I could have gotten a seven figures number three days ago, but not the conditions I believe Gabrielle Lewyn will accept."

"Which ones?" she interjected before feeling adrenalin draining from her nervous system. Two adolescent surfboarders unconcerned how they might interrupt the walkers' stride almost collided with Tony who with a firm jerk hauled Lydia back in time to avoid a collision. He barked a nasty swearword, which the kids showed no sign of hearing.

"Everybody I've talked with had the same response. Wonderful… but."

"But what, friend?"

"But this is a political hot potato. They see major conflict with the Catholic Church. Nobody wants to do battle with those on High. Yet the story of discovery, especially the scrap between Father Benoir and

Timothy Matternly, and their deaths…all dynamite stuff for the box office. This is particularly intriguing because it's true. Absolutely fabulous material for the screen. It might be possible to start preliminary work in six months. I can get ten out of ten producers to bid for it this afternoon."

"Why fear the Catholic Church? Tony, my old friend and modestly good lover in bed, don't bullshit me. Why?"

He remained silent for a spell, glancing out to gentle waves rolling to the beach. "It's got to do with religious sensibilities. The script attacks the fundamental doctrine of Jesus as God, or God's preferred son. Hollywood wants box office receipts, not a religious war. To put it simply, Jesus is too rooted in Christian theology. A Hollywood movie, no matter how sensitively directed and lavishly produced, is bound to awaken sleeping sensitivities. If you think the Latin Church will be annoyed, think about the Protestant churches. They don't have the pomp and ceremony of Catholicism, but they're fanatic believers in the divinity of Jesus."

"This is no time for timidity," she replied.

"Personally, I agree," he responded, "but we must avoid appearing as bulls in a china shop. The project could backfire and come to bite us."

"Did anyone mention mediation?"

"Of course. Like bringing in Cardinal Brandini of Los Angeles and giving Christian authorities a consulting role."

"That's censorship." Lydia almost growled.

"You said it, but I think you're right."

"Gabby will never accept that."

"If she's a bit flexible, she'll be a very wealthy woman."

"I already told you she isn't interested in money. After all she's endured with the fragment, she only wants the world to know what she knows. And I don't believe she lusts for recognition. She sent me here to sell an idea, not to get an Academy Award."

That night, Lydia and Tony dined in a local West Hollywood Mexican restaurant. They munched on too many tortilla chips and imbibed a good quantity of Dos Equis beer. Tony moved from opposite Lydia to sit beside her, enjoying the warmth of her body nudged against his. Conversation centered upon how to produce a movie about a deeply emotional theme, one that purported to be about events that really happened, not about an imaginary tale told to impress the box office.

Tony had hoped to be invited to stay the evening with Lydia at the Marriott. That didn't occur. Disappointed while driving home, he concluded that time had produced changes in his old friend. She was as delicious as ever but had lost some of her earlier lust. What a damn shame!

Chapter Nine

Kar'ine's Hezbollah associates in Damascus were worried about her. They were originally Beirut merchants who, with their Hezbollah Party cohorts, had followed the course of Islamic wars in support of the Ba'ath government in Syria. Originally a military cadre organized to fight Israel, and after two disastrous wars with the Israeli Defense Force, Hezbollah morphed into an opposition party focused on improving living conditions for Palestinians living in Lebanon. To pay hemorrhaging expenses, Hezbollah peddled its military and financial expertise as mercenaries to the beleaguered Syrian government. That worked to Israel's benefit because while occupied in Syria, Hezbollah fighters remained quiet on the northern frontier with Lebanon. And equally significant, they focused on fighting Syrian insurgents and refrained from striking at Israel along the Golan Heights.

Kar'ine's Hezbollah associates found lucrative employment in Damascus as financial managers. Omar Miodhat Hamad, Mohammad Ahmad Hijazi, Yahia abu Mustafa, and Salah Sabr al-Ejla wisely avoided open competition with their Syrian patrons when buying and selling archeological treasures. Kar'ine proved to be perfect for their trade. In essence they sold their wares to her, then took a substantial fee for moving these purchases to Beirut. Only Mohammad Ahmad Hijazi, among the four, had actually slept with her and that amounted to a one-night-stand in the five-star Omayyad Hotel.

After 9 p.m. Kar'ine arrived at Al Khawali a quiet unassuming restaurant in Damascus' Old Quarter selected by Mohammad Ahmad Hijazi. Seated before the others arrived, Kar'ine ordered a Jordanian Carakale beer and peered nervously at the *bahra*, a fountain spewing a double stream of water into the air and retrieving the excess in an illuminated pond. The customary Arab salads and mounds of pita were set on engraved brass Syrian tables.

Mohammad Ahmad Hijazi marched immediately to Kar'ine's table and before she could acknowledge his presence he slid onto a seat beside her. She greeted him, "I presume your colleagues are en route."

Mohammad reached in front of her and held his posture there for an extra moment before whispering, "Kar'ine, you know how fluid the military situation is these days. My friends are not coming. They've disappeared and I fear for the worst."

"Problems with the government?"

"Several antiquity dealers have been arrested. It started happening when news seeped out about the catacombs blown up by ISIL troops in Palmyra. Government officials wanted to control this traffic but learned they were too late. Robbers had already cleaned subterranean caverns exposed by ISIL explosives. Yahia abu Mustafa and Salah Sabr al-Ejla are missing."

"Omar Miodhat Hamad?"

"Haven't heard from him. He doesn't answer his cell phone."

Two Bedouin servants waited for a pause in the conversation to set a supplementary table, ready for whatever their guests would order from the menu. This gave Kar'ine a moment to gather control of her emotions that for an instant surged out of control.

"You're acquainted with Mahdi Ata' al Rahman?" Mohammad filled an awkward moment.

She didn't want anyone to learn about her unfortunate relationship with the Aleppo dealer, but an immediate evaluation told her that holding back was a poor idea. "Yes. We've done business in the past. Is there something I should know about him?"

Mohammad received a menu but hardly eyed it before saying, "Your friend has been spreading rumors about you. He claims you and your late husband owe him a great sum of money. Whether true or not, this is not in your interests, Kar'ine Salik. Government officials are quite aware of your work here and they're uncomfortable with your style of business. That you're a woman, the surviving wife of Dr. Salik, doesn't help. It wouldn't take much for Mahdi Ata' al Rahman to put you out of business. And that, I'm sorry to say, equates to arrest. You're quite vulnerable here. Your friends in the United States are too far away to help."

Kar'ine processed this disclosure and reposted with a quick question. "Should I be worried about my safety?"

Mohammad said nothing until she repeated the question. Eventually he answered, "Yes."

"Then I should leave Damascus?"

"Excuse me for intruding into your private business, but your life is more important. If you move quickly I believe I can get you safely to Beirut."

"What about you? You're respected and needed by the government."

"True but that's not very satisfying. If they come after my colleagues it's only a matter of time before they'll knock on my door."

"And suppose I decide to remain at least for another week?"

"A bad idea. Nobody has control here. My colleagues and I are hired guns. Our welcome is in constant flux."

"I can pay Mahdi Ata' al Rahman a good sum to quiet him."

"His inquiries have already spread too far. I don't like losing a good source of income any better than you. But I must be practical. Perhaps when things settle down in this country my colleagues and I, if they're still alive, can resume normal business. I have a car ready to drive to Beirut tomorrow at two o'clock. Come with me, Kar'ine."

Dinner started but ended abruptly on a sour theme. Mohammad Ahmad Hijazi promised to swing by the Omayyad Hotel at 1:45 p.m. to transport her over the Lebanese frontier to Beirut. If, between now and then, she decided to remain in Damascus she would need to employ new transfer agents.

* * * * *

Kar'ine was forced to reconsider the threat that Mahdi Ata' al Rahman presented. For her own sake she couldn't afford to brush him off. True, she had found him to be physically repulsive, but the fact was that less desirable dealers had migrated themselves into her bed. When she elected to sleep with her customers it was always her choice, not theirs. Not a single one had ever compelled her to share her body with them.

When Mahdi Ata' al Rahman returned to the Damascus Omayyad, she told him, "I am consulting with my bank to help you and your family. But know without any ambiguity that I will not allow you in my bed to dishonor your family. Married men never think how their infidelities injure their wives. And the loose women who slip between the sheets with cheating husbands compound this misery. You have no idea the pain this causes. No, Mahdi Ata' al Rahman, you will never, never share my bed."

"You misjudge me, Madam. I was married, rather happily too as a matter of fact, but two years ago my wife, Ghaaliya, died from ovarian cancer. To maintain my household and help with the children, I employ a full-time servant from the Philippines."

"My apologies, please. And my condolences for the loss of Ghaaliya."

There was no doubt in Kar'ine's mind how officials in Damascus or the new Islamic rulers in Raqqa would abuse her. Still she held her ground saying, "Go to whatever authorities you choose, but then you will never receive a cent for your losses. Come back here tomorrow morning at 9 a.m. sharp. Cash is scheduled to arrive from Beirut early in the morning. I may have some funds not already committed."

As all Arab merchants, she had developed the craft of reading slight movements of the eyelids and a softening of the lips. That, she interpreted, as a signal of his pleasure in retrieving at least a part of his losses. In his mind he must have already accepted a full loss, only to be encouraged by the prospect of getting a portion back. Aware that he had not insisted on defining the exact sum, she added, "And when you come bring your Palmyrene fragment."

That took him off-guard. "I've been truthful and acknowledged to you it is not original. It is old but not original. Why are you interested in a mere copy?"

Here she manufactured the beginnings of a faint smile, the first warmth between them. "I'm not sure. Curiosity about this Silk Road correspondence. I thought I understood ancient commercial ties with Syria, but letters between the East and West are something entirely new. This might be a welcome addition to my education."

* * * * *

Mahdi Ata' al Rahman was prompt at 9 a.m. the following day, a characteristic Kar'ine noted to be rare in Arab merchants, but then she understood him to be desperate for money. She received his call from the hotel lobby announcing his arrival and willingness to meet her in the coffee shop.

"No," she said, "The cash has arrived and I don't want to expose it in public. Come to my room. 1104. Don't let anyone see you. I'm counting on your discretion."

Shortly afterward, a soft knock on the hotel door announced Mahdi. She unfastened a chain lock and peered into the corridor. The antiquities dealer was smartly dressed in an expensive business suit with a freshly laundered white shirt and fashionable green necktie. She could see the surprise in his eyes as if he expected to find her in her customary gray business attire and hijab, certainly not in a light blue silk robe covering cream-colored pajamas. Her chestnut-red hair was uncovered. As always when in private quarters she was barefoot.

The hotel staff had already delivered breakfast coffee, which she poured into a large china cup and asked if he wished cream. They sat beside a round table where she opened conversation with what she knew to be uppermost in his mind. "Today, Mahdi Ata' al Rahman, I will repay a part of the losses incurred in business with my husband. Despite negative talk about my family on the street, our honor remains sacred. I want no stain on the Salik memory. I am prepared to give you $65,000 for your losses, if and only if you pledge in writing there will be no future claims. This is a one-time offer. You understand?"

She studied his face for a reaction and found it mixed. It was probably more than he anticipated, but less than hoped. "A mere symbol of my loss," he manufactured a sigh, and with his palms opened he was holding out for more. "My expenses…"

Kar'ine expected him to barter for more and waited through a charged moment before elevating her offer to what she held in her mind to be the last. "$75,000. My best. And not a bad one for someone in your position."

He ran that through his mind, saying nothing while slowly nodding his head in acceptance.

"And the Palmyrene document? You've brought it with you, I presume."

He leaned forward to a briefcase set on the floor beside his feet. "Of course. Are you still interested in buying?"

"I must look at it first."

He retrieved an airtight transparent envelope and handed it to Kar'ine, who in turn snatched reading glasses from a pocket in her housecoat. The document was about three-quarters the size on a standard letter, written in Aramaic script.

Kar'ine could not read this dialect of Palmyrene yet quickly determined that she wanted the document, but not at the price she believe Mahdi Ata' al Rahman would ask. "Clearly, a copy, but I would like it for my private collection. Not for resale to my patrons." she said. "Unfortunately, after paying you $75,000 from private funds, I am at a loss for more resources."

Mahdi was adept at employing silence at a critical point in negotiations. Eventually he said, "You look ravishing this morning, Kar'ine Salik, especially in your sleeping attire. You know that I have long nourished an appetite for you."

"I know," she returned, her tone businesslike and devoid of intimacy. "I am prepared to make you an offer. This is non-negotiable. The Palmyrene document for thirty minutes in bed with me. A deal, Mahdi?"

"When?"

"Now," she was quick. "I have a very demanding schedule today. If you agree, go to the bathroom and remove your trousers. I will be in the bed naked, the way men like to be with their women. But thirty minutes only. If you can't complete your business in a half-hour, you're not the man I thought you were. The clock begins the moment you exit from the bathroom. Agreed?"

He stood in preparation.

"First, sign the document waving further claims on your losses from my husband. While you are undressing I will put $75,000 beside it. The Palmyrene document stays on this table. You may leave after thirty minutes with your money. And the letter remains with me. Agreed?"

There was frog in his throat as he tried to vocalize his consent.

Kar'ine's professional acumen transferred from business to the bed. Though her organs felt not the slightest tinge of passion, she pretended as though she were enjoying the experience, all the while allowing her eyes to monitor an electric alarm clock on the bed stand.

For Mahdi Ata' al Rahman thirty minutes elapsed faster than he anticipated. He wasn't prepared to stop, yet to the second Kar'ine pulled away and left the bed. An instant later she snatched the signed waiver and the Palmyrene document from the table and marched toward the bathroom, leaving a bewildered lover still in the bed.

Before closing the door behind her, she barked, "Take your money and be gone Mahdi Ata' al Rahman."

* * * * *

Itamar wrote a letter of resignation as Director of Israel Antiquities, but knowing it was not final until actually delivered, placed it in an unsealed envelope and carefully tucked it beneath his desk blotter. He knew Gabby would certainly fight him about it. Still, the political hacks in the Israeli Knesset, people he had come to regard not only as incompetent but also self-righteous petty thieves, had driven him to a point of despair. He had done his duty for his country; now let some other chump ride the bucking horse of state. The emotional exertion of deciding on his future placed pressure on his bladder, commanding him to relieve himself.

He knew he was a bad mood and that it was no time to make such a momentous decision. Standing before the urinal in the Men's Room, his thoughts wandered to a future free from politics. A university job either in Israel or abroad, while sleepy in comparison with running the Department of Antiquities, had its merits.

He raised his chin to regard an image in the mirror above the urinal and found, to his surprise, a man standing behind him as if waiting to use the facility. He was no stranger, yet the last person he would have thought to encounter in the Department's restroom.

"*Boker Or*, Good Morning," he greeted Itamar.

The presence of Porcupine could only mean bad news. "Is Kar'ine dead?" he asked, dipping his chin and after adjusting his fly lifted terrified eyes to scrutinize Porcupine.

"No. I told you countless times not to worry. We would do the best that we could to protect her. And we did."

"What do you mean *did*? She's okay?" the level of his voice rose with a mounting sense of hope.

Porcupine answered, "Better than that, *haver*, friend. Kar'ine Salik is alive and well and no longer in Syria. She left day before yesterday by car along with a Hezbollah colleague. She's now comfortably enjoying freedom in the Philadelphia Hotel in Beirut. We're going to move her out as soon as it's safe."

"I'll go fetch her," Itamar offered.

The smidgen of warmth on Porcupine's face disappeared. "You'll do nothing of the kind. Before you get your mitts on her she must be debriefed."

"I can get a diplomatic pass from the United Nations to collect her in Lebanon."

"I doubt it, and certainly don't advise trying. Be patient and you'll have her back."

"In Israel?"

"If she wants to come here."

"You're not going to welch again about the promised permanent visa, are you? You broke your previous pledge not once but twice."

"No problem with the visa. It's hers if and when she wants to be in Israel. But, I must warn you, it's not a done deal that she wants this. I shouldn't have to explain why a Muslim woman would hesitate living in a Jewish state."

"Where are you taking her from Beirut?"

"I'm not sure my superiors have selected a place. She'll fly out commercially, but we don't want to alert Hezbollah operatives who by now know that their own colleague drove her from Damascus. We don't want her to use her Syrian passport."

"I have a right to meet her wherever that might be."

"Sorry, Iti, we don't deal with rights. When she's fully debriefed, then and only then we'll let you know where."

"I think she'll come to Israel."

"You're entitled to your views but it's better for you to let this salacious woman go. I know character and I know a besotted man when I see one. We know you and Gabrielle Lewyn are back together. That, my friend, makes good sense. I don't share your emotions, but I advise you to cherish what you have. The world is filled with tribes. And Kar'ine Salik, no matter what she's done for Israel, is not a member of ours. And never will become one."

Porcupine cracked the projection room door to evaluate foot traffic in the corridor and, when he observed no one there, seized the moment to swish through. Itamar followed, but somehow *the snake*, as he thought of this government agent, seemed to have slithered away unseen.

* * * * *

Porcupine could have returned Kar'ine into Israel through a frontier gate separating northern Israel from Lebanon. But to avoid the possibility of a slip-up before she crossed, he sent her by Aegean Airlines to Athens from where he intended to personally escort her back to Israel. For that purpose he brought a full-length black cotton dress, heavy brown stockings, a jet-black dyed wig and babushka meant to disguise her as a middle-aged observant woman. He, on the other hand, had allowed his salt-and-pepper beard to grow, wore an expensive three-quarter length worsted woolen jacket and a black Stetson hat, frequently used by the well-to-do Orthodox.

From Ben Gurion Airport outside Tel Aviv a non-descript government car drove them to Jerusalem, more specifically to the Orthodox district of Mea Sharim, a 19th Century enclave dedicated to the preservation of ultra-observant living. Once there, Kar'ine was taken to a secured apartment rented by the government intelligence agency.

Beside Porcupine there were three men dressed like observant Jews, with decent but groomed beards, white-and-black clothing, and black leather shoes. None introduced themselves before settling into desks as interrogators. Porcupine invited Kar'ine to remove her heavy clothing and to use the facilities to freshen up, after which a series of queries had been prepared for her.

As the proceedings began it was clear that Porcupine would not be asking the questions, though he sat behind the others and prepared on the table a legal pad for notes.

"Call me Danny," the senior interrogator began in a friendly, off-the-cuff manner. "From the outset, please understand that we know there may be personal things you don't want to share with us. But whatever you can, it would be helpful. We believe you were able to observe things in Syria that are closed to us for obvious reasons. Since 1967 our border with Syria has been a relatively quiet, non-eventful frontier that we'd like to maintain. And of course, we don't control what's transpiring in Syria these days. Hezbollah's friendship with Iran is worrying."

Kar'ine intervened, "You know many of my business associates are Hezbollah. You also know, of course, that Hezbollah has its fighters, largely well trained and armed with Iranian weapons. They've become mercenaries who, I can assure you, wouldn't lift a finger for the Damascus government if they weren't paid handsomely."

"Did you deal or come in contact with the military arm of Hezbollah?"

"Not directly. I dealt with Hezbollah advisors who were in Damascus to manage government funds. They were originally Lebanese merchants skilled at handling money. I found them very useful moving assets from the Bemo Bank in Beirut to Damascus and Aleppo. But more importantly, once I took possession of expensive artifacts I needed to move them safely out of the war zone to Beirut where the buyers took responsibility for shipping them to Europe and America."

"We take it your arrangements were satisfactory," added Danny. "No problems with your associates?"

"On the contrary. I'm an Arab woman. Most Arab men don't like doing business with women. But my Lebanese associates were exemplary. There were many opportunities to cheat me, but they never did, at least not as far as I know. They could have stolen one or more shipments of invaluable artifacts, but they professionally refrained."

"Did they report to higher Hezbollah authorities in Syria? Or Lebanon?"

"Yes, but I met only three high-ranking officials. Two dinners in their company. The hosts provided names but they were no more genuine than Danny or Porcupine."

"Do you recall the pseudonyms?"

"No. In my trade it is not wise to refer to anyone except those with whom you're doing direct business. As you probably know from Itamar Arad, dealing in antiquities is dangerous. Not just for me but for anybody dealing with stolen property. Hezbollah businessmen were not exempt. Two of my people were arrested: Mohammad Ahmad Hijazi and Salah Sabr al-Ejla. Another, Yahia Abu Mustafa, was deported back to Lebanon." She watched as the interrogators wrote down the names given on their legal pads.

"Who helped you escape?"

She didn't respond immediately, curled her lips and eventually said, "That's personal. I had good friends in a difficult place. If you fail to hide my identity, they will face an uncertain future. Not just in Syria but in Lebanon, or any Muslim country where they choose to do business. I know Hezbollah is your enemy; understand please, it is not mine."

The Israeli interrogators looked at each other to evaluate this response. Danny glanced at Porcupine before stating, "But you may eventually stay in our neck of the woods. You can appreciate what we must do to stay alive."

"Of course I can. As a Shia Muslim, although not very religious, I understand what it feels like to be surrounded by people who hate you."

"Of course not," Danny interrupted, acknowledging that they had wandered off subject. He returned to a list of questions before him. They ranged from observations of military hardware to the routes used for transporting Syrian artifacts to Lebanon: the turnover of Hezbollah merchants, the restaurants and clubs they frequented. What vehicles they did they drive? Wives? Girlfriends? Recreational activities? Vacation time with families in Lebanon? Europe? Travel through the warzones of Syria?

After five hours of a questioning, Porcupine had Kar'ine don her Orthodox clothing to take her to the Kings Hotel just east of Jerusalem's Independence Park with instructions not to contact Itamar. She should expect another long day of questions, after which she would be free to contact whomever she wanted.

The second day of debriefing was shorter and lighter than the first. It became clear that her interrogators enjoyed being in the company of an erudite, attractive woman and had developed an appreciation for her business in a warzone, a business they came to understand brought her a substantial wealth. When the meeting ended they all shook her hand with sincere wishes that she would decide to live in Israel.

That was on Porcupine's mind when driving her back to her hotel. "You can be assured that Israel will keep its pledge to you. If you wish, you'll have your visa for permanent residence. Itamar has spoken to me about finding you a suitable job to utilize your skills. We'll do what we can."

She replied, "I didn't tell the others because it's none of their business, but I can tell you now that I've just been offered a job as associate-curator at the J Paul Getty Museum in California. Some of the people I represented in Syria liked my work and offered me a staff position. I'm tempted. Never been to America. From what I read, modern Arab women do well there."

"There's much in this country you haven't seen," Porcupine said. "You're earned a place in Israel.'"

She sighed aloud. "Yes, but this is a Jewish nation and I'm not Jewish. I've spent too much of my life as an outsider. No matter your courtesy to me, I'll always be an outsider here. From what I read, the United States is entirely different."

"Itamar will be disappointed. He's very fond of you. But of course, you already know that."

In the offloading zone of the King's Hotel, she replied, "I know. For me Itamar is the most desirable man I've ever known. But like with everything there's an imperfection. Two major issues for me."

"Oh," Porcupine turned off the ignition and arched his right arm over the passenger seat to let her finish the idea. "Only two?"

"Itamar belongs to another woman and not some statuesque beauty with hummus for brains. I'd be an outright fool to compete with a woman as appealing as Gabrielle Lewyn. I'm impulsive and risk-taking but I'm no fool."

He nodded his concurrence with this evaluation before asking, "And the second."

"I'm an Arab woman. Arabs and Jews have common ancestors but we've been fighting each other for three thousand years. Itamar is a Jew and I am not. In this part of the world, you know as well I that blood runs deeper than tolerance. You wouldn't do the work you do if you didn't believe that."

For that, Porcupine could add no wisdom. He attempted to create a worthy response but came up flat. Instead he changed the subject, "Give away the Orthodox clothing. You won't need it anymore. You're free to contact Itamar now. You will call him, won't you?"

She wagged her head negatively. "I don't think so. It would only stir old embers. But I would like to know where I can find Gabrielle Lewyn."

"I will arrange a meeting with her if you wish."

"No thanks. That's not what I had in mind. Nothing arranged between us. If you can, just give me her schedule in the next day or so. I'll find her on my own."

* * * * *

Porcupine called Kar'ine at the Kings Hotel to relate what his staff had told him about Gabby. Once back in Jerusalem from Wadi Qelt, she had resumed her work at the Shrine of the Book and on Tuesdays and Thursdays at 11 a.m. conducted a guided tour through the Timothy Matternly Annex, explaining the contribution his discoveries had made to Dead Sea scholarship. That was exactly what Kar'ine wanted to know.

* * * * *

While waiting to encounter Gabby at the Shrine of the Book on Thursday, Kar'ine improved her wardrobe in the city's retail center, resumed an exercise regime in the hotel gym and spend time walking Jerusalem's byways, visiting the Old City and drinking coffee in the street-side cafes. She ate familiar Middle Eastern food in Arab restaurants.

On Thursday, dressed in a summer lavender dress purchased the day before and carrying a black vinyl business folder, she took the opportunity to visit the main display of Dead Sea documents in the circular rotunda of the Shrine of the Book where these priceless fragments of First Century Jewish history were exhibited. Almost the entire scroll of the Book of Isaiah was displayed before her eyes, significant because this manuscript from the First Century of the Common Era predated the oldest authoritative Masoretic text from the Ninth Century and with few exceptions was identical. That had profound implications for the authenticity of the Old Testament. Kar'ine was familiar with the ancient Aramaic script of this document but was unfamiliar with the Hebrew. As a student of Syrian antiquities, she marveled at the window these Dead Sea scrolls opened to life in Judea during the explosive First Century.

At 10:45 a.m. she strode through a connecting corridor to the Timothy Matternly exhibition annex that Gabrielle Lewyn had founded and helped finance in Matternly's memory. There, in modest but tasteful displays were fragments her deceased boyfriend had rescued from Cave XII in Qumran. Showcases illustrated how multiple fragments, some of single words, some of individual letters and others more complex structures, such as phrases and multiple verses, were later reconstructed.

Kar'ine returned to the connecting corridor as she watched a group of twenty European archeology students cluster together awaiting Dr. Lewyn's presentation. She was late, but the students entertained themselves chatting about the exhibitions. When Gabby finally arrived through a side door, Kar'ine observed an athletic stride that corresponded with a lean figure. The natural simplicity of her facial features struck her. Behind thin designer spectacles were warm penetrating eyes. Especially deep dimples enlarged as she welcomed the students and began explaining how the Matternly wing of the Shrine came about and how it supplements the museum's main exhibition.

Kar'ine held back an appropriate distance to study Gabby, who remained unaware of her presence. The moment was filled with both sadness and elation. Deep in her woman's heart she had hoped to find a dumpy rival who shared a mutual love of antiquity. But Gabby presented nothing of that. She was unpretentiously elegant. Kar'ine was unable to understand her own reaction because instead of slipping into raw, uncontrolled jealousy, her spirits rose as she measured her competitor.

Kar'ine had cultivated a hard, realistic persona publicly despising human weakness, especially sentimental tears. Yet as she observed Gabby her eyes became moist. If she loved Itamar as she knew she did, wouldn't any lover want what was best for the beloved? By any measure, abandoning such an appealing woman as Gabrielle for an Arab stranger was not in his interest.

Gabby obviously enjoyed the students' enthusiasm, mixing her presentation with both declarations and questions. Moving counterclockwise around the museum floor she described both Matternly's dramatic discovery in Cave XII and the way Rabbi Zechariah Schreiber deciphered the fragmentary material utilizing Tim Matternly's computer code. Before the appropriate back-lit display cases she spoke of the monastic Frist Century society depicted in the deciphered texts. A full display case was devoted to the letter written by the Roman procurator describing a school for prophets in the Judean Desert, and how Tim Matternly was later slain at this location, most likely by local Bedouin, a crime never satisfactorily explained by the Israel police.

For the last, she held back a cabinet display of eleven Hebrew proper names, most probably a roster of students who attended this school for prophets. She attempted to paint a picture of a prophetic profession common in the First Century. "Prophecy, in those days, was not understood as a talent infused by God into a recipient, but as the result of disciplined training to become a proper spokesman for Deity."

The cadre of students was much animated by the subject. Individuals threw questions at Gabby that she answered with obvious acumen. Finally she introduced a question that had not been raised, "And what would you say if I told you there was one more name on that student roster that until a few days ago had never been revealed?"

Nobody said anything until Gabby responded, "Let me give you a clue. You all saw the YouTube posting of the name *Yeshu*, didn't you? Of course. Everybody saw it. And just about everybody learned from authoritative sources that it was another Piltdown Man hoax. Right?"

"Wrong," she responded rhetorically. "There's been a major breakthrough. That *Yeshu* Fragment never was and isn't now a phony. It was real and it exists safely somewhere in the Vatican. Someday, I know not when, but someday that name *Yeshu*, son of Joseph, will be displayed here in this museum along with the other eleven names. Why? Because the *Yeshu* name was discovered in the Qumran cave along with the eleven proper names you see here! It may astound you to learn that Jesus had been a student at this School for Prophets!"

"Can you prove it?" snapped one of the students.

Here Gabby was less enthusiastic. "I think so, but there are always holes in any proof. I've just learned a new fact from a Fifth Century document surviving from Palmyra in Syria. It was part of correspondence between the Eastern and Western branches of the Byzantine Orthodox Christian Church. In a newly discovered copy of a letter from Palmyra to Jerusalem, Jesus is described not as the Son of God but as a trained prophet with fresh ideas about what God wanted for his people. This missive is so fresh it hasn't yet been shared with the academic community."

Multiple questions erupted which Gabby patiently fielded until the students' guide declared the tour ended in favor of a rendezvous for lunch in the nearby Israel Museum cafeteria. When the group finally exited through the corridor leading back to the Shrine of the Book, Kar'ine held back, watching as Gabby prepared to leave through the same side door from which she had entered.

She suddenly marched swiftly forward and planted a restraining hand on Gabby's shoulder. It forced Gabby to wheel about and face a woman in a beige Muslim *hijab* covering chestnut-red hair. For a long moment the two women stood in silence absorbing the image of the other. Tears that had begun earlier in Kar'ine's eyes now streamed freely along her cheeks. Gabby remembered this woman from the bazaar in Istanbul, but over the course of months the mental image had tarnished. Suddenly refreshed, the women appeared more beautiful than in memory, the woman she had come to believe had turned Itamar's heart. She couldn't account for what she did next, but it seemed in response to the fact that Kar'ine was obviously crying. Gabby grasped her in a prolonged and emotional bear hug, a reunion of sisters long separated.

"I remember you from the *shook*," Gabby eventually said.

"Yes," Kar'ine replied. "You posed as an antiquities dealer from Chicago, if my memory serves me, but I could see you didn't know much about Syrian artifacts. When you described a man you were looking for in Istanbul, I knew it was Itamar."

"You fled from the shop before we could talk."

Kar'ine's head nodded affirmatively providing time to fashion her response. "In confusion, I believe. Or more probably, in shame. It was then that I understood how I had fallen. My husband hurt me by bringing home women to make love in our own home, sometimes in our marriage bed. I can't describe the humiliation. I hated these women with all the Arab passion I could muster, and you Jews know how bitter that Arab passion can be. Then, when I met you in the bazaar and you were looking for Itamar, I understood how I was no better than the women I detested."

Gabby thought about Kar'ine's confession, running the turn of events in her mind while keeping her eyes planted on Kar'ine's. What happened next was beyond her capacity to rationalize. It was the voice of intuition, not reason, which moved her. She pulled from her pocket a handkerchief always stowed there for a drippy nose and gently patted dry the moisture of Kar'ine's tears.

"We are sisters," she whispered. "In love with the same man."

"True, but he is yours not mine. I hurt so much from my life in Aleppo that I had lost control over myself. I had no right to take what was yours. I apologize. Believe me, Sister, it was one night and one night only. Never more. One night of shameful weakness."

Gabby's head continued to nod. "I've thought about it often and concluded there was no purpose to confront Itamar. What happened in the past is over. You and I are historians and we both know how history eclipses itself. Will you see Iti?"

"I think not. I'm going to Los Angeles where I've been offered a job. Israel doesn't need a woman like me. Here I will always be an outsider.

They hugged again, this time holding for an even longer period than before. When they finally broke, it was Kar'ine who sniffled and said, "Oh, Gabrielle, I almost forgot." She opened the leather folder brought in a Jerusalem shop the day before and snatched an air-sealed see-through envelope. Inside was a three-quarter-page of Palmyrene Aramaic. "I brought his from Damascus for you."

Gabby looked to read a few known words of Aramaic. "What is it?"

"You just mentioned Christian letters between Palmyra and Jerusalem. I think this is part of that correspondence. Religious questions asked by eastern Christians to the Orthodox Church in Jerusalem."

"Have we stumbled into the same thing? What you bring must be very valuable. I'll request funds from the Israel Museum to pay for it."

"Absolutely not. It's my gift to you. If you wish to place it in this museum that would be fine, but I had you in mind when I acquired it."

"But you must have paid a lot of money."

Kar'ine's mind flash briefly to the half-hour she had spent in bed with *Mahdi Ata' al Rahman.* "It cost me nothing but a small piece of my pride. I owe you at least this."

Gabby's eyes stayed fixed on the document. "I will see it has a proper home in the museum library for other scholars to study."

Kar'ine turned to retreat along the corridor to the main display in the Shrine, but Gabby stopped her, "It never occurred to me I would meet a woman like you. And I'm grateful for this document. Another piece in a complex puzzle about early Christianity."

Kar'ine's lips touched Gabby's cheek. An exotic and rare fragrance from the East emanated from her skin before she turned and headed down the corridor.

Chapter Ten

The fact that Kar'ine had not made contact caused Itamar to believe that perhaps Porcupine was right; that after all they had gone through she didn't want to live in Israel. Yet he couldn't accommodate for his own feelings. Experts often said that one could not possess feelings about two individuals at the same time, but in his case they were dead wrong. He did. It wasn't something he had chosen; it had been thrust upon him. And it didn't feel unnatural. He was certain that Gabby knew or at least suspected. But, as always, she possessed the good horse sense not to make it into a confrontation.

Itamar didn't like the way Porcupine treated him but realized his limitations in dealing with an official protected by the secrecy of his own government. From his personal experience in the Antiquities Agency he knew that trying to combat Mossad was futile, somewhat akin to batting the air in order to kill a mosquito. There was nothing to do but wait until Porcupine was finished with Kar'ine, then wherever she might be, he'd tell Gabby what he was doing and rush immediately to see her.

But even after she was released by Porcupine she made no attempt at seeing him.

* * * * *

In part, it was Prime Minister Sonnenberg who eased Itamar's anxiety. Once the press got its teeth into implications of Father Benoir's memoirs, the YouTube posting came into focus. The Israel Government needed to stop calling it a fraud. The Prime Minister had no direct communications from the Vatican but he knew the Holy See was as embarrassed as Jerusalem.

The Old Man, as comrades often referred to him, commanded Itamar, "It's time the Church of Rome and the Government of Israel get their acts together, and better in unison than operating separately. I want you to go to Rome and get this matter settled with the Secretary of State Cardinal…Cardinal whatever his fuckin' name is…"

"Donaldo Cardinal Fornetti," Itamar added.

"Yes. Let that sonavabitch know we're not playing around with this issue anymore. The Vatican has possession of the fragment, and it's their fuckin' problem, not Israel's. And by the way, I've decided to let Rabbi Lewyn off the hook. My Palestinian spies tell me that professional goons from Bosnia were looking for her, but fortunately we arrested and later deported them. Another embarrassment for Rome. You tell Rabbi Lewyn for me that despite my big mouth I never sent hoodlums to injure her. Didn't do it then and won't do it now. In fact, she's done this nation a big service. As far as I'm concerned, the gag rule is off. For you and for her. Since the public now knows the fragment is genuine, you can say whatever you want. And I wouldn't mind if Rabbi Lewyn can persuade the Vatican to exhibit the fragment in the Shrine of the Book. I'm not much of an historian, but this piece of parchment is most significantly displayed along with the other discoveries of Professor Matternly."

"When do you wish me to make contact with Rome?"

"As soon as you can arrange it. Let them know our patience is finished. The Church has its problems and I have mine. Time to move on."

* * * * *

For Itamar the unfolding events were sobering. Now that things appeared to be resolved, he acknowledged that he had treated Gabby badly. Since he was flying to Italy on state business it might be an opportune time to rebuild what had been broken in their relationship. They had begun their romance in Tuscany—the perfect venue to restore what was temporarily lost. The only impediment was Kar'ine's possible residence in Israel. If in the slim chance she decided to make Israel her home, he wanted to welcome her.

Persuading Gabby to join him in Italy was easier than he thought. It turned out that prior to receiving an order from the Prime Minister, Gabby had fielded a similar request from Father Sebastian. Out of a job but not excommunicated, the Vatican had ordered him to the Holy See for consultations, along with a pledge to pay his traveling expenses.

Sebastian, who had become more resilient during the past months, was nervous. The Church held the keys to his future and experience taught that it was not a kindly master when offended. Jesuits ruled the chicken coop and they had never been overly friendly toward Dominicans. Father Benoir Matteau's memoirs were certain to cause headaches for the papacy.

For support, Sebastian invited Gabby to help him in the Italian capital. No one knew more about the history of the *Yeshu* Fragment than she, which made her into a valuable ally when being interrogated by Church theologians and lawyers.

"I'll need you beside me at the Inquisition," he said. "Today, they can't torture me, but I don't expect sympathetic treatment. A lowly Dominican priest in the midst of Jesuit wolves hasn't got much of a chance. You know what they do to fallen priests?"

"No. But I have a fertile imagination."

"We get posted to remote jungles where we're either butchered by the natives or we catch a terrible disease and die in our humble parishes from insufficient medicine. Not a very dignified end for a priest-scholar like me."

"And it won't happen," Gabby stated with powerful affirmation.

"And you can pull miracles for me?"

"My beloved priest," she responded, "there are some things worth fighting for in this miserable world and many more things not worthy of the energy. But you're worth it. If you hadn't hidden me at Wadi Qelt, assassins might have slit my throat. And if you hadn't believed in Father Benoir, I'd have no way to prove the *Yeshu* Fragment is genuine. No, my friend, you're quite worth it. And I intend to fight, even the lofty Pope if I must."

* * * * *

Father Sebastian was right, he wasn't invited to Rome for friendly consultations. At the inquest there were four Vatican lawyers and three official Church scholars. Sebastian was not afforded the privilege of legal counsel, yet Gabby was allowed to attend as a silent observer, not even as a professional witness.

The inquest began with inquiries about how Father Benoir got involved with cave robbers in Qumran and his partnership with Professor Timothy Matternly. Much interest was devoted to what went sour in their relationship. Why did Benoir return to Israel illegally and why were the Israel police reticent about investigating his murder?

Then it got personal. Was Sebastian's relationship with Father Benoir homosexual, or was it purely professional interest? What moved him to dedicate so much time to Benoir's memoirs, and did the Ecole's directors approve of his personal passion to reconstruct Benoir's work? Once he had deciphered these notes, why did he share them with Rabbi Gabrielle Lewyn? More importantly, once he became aware that the *Yeshu* Fragment was real, why didn't he disclose what he knew to his superiors? Or the Vatican?

The Reverend Monsignor Erwin Nebdal, Dean of the Teutonic College of Sacred Archeology and Ecclesiastic History, who presided over the first day of questioning, revealed that the Church was not pleased with Sebastian's behavior. He had set a bad example of clerical discipline and gone well beyond his station to be involved in such a momentous episode. Far from delivering a significant service for the Church, Sebastian had performed a terrible disservice by disrupting a delicate balance in understanding of Christian history.

Gabby was infuriated by the ingratitude expressed by Monsignor Nebdal's coterie of sycophantic lawyers. Their disrespect for a talented scholar who had served the Church prompted her to stand and voice her condemnation for the tone and content of the inquest. She was so emotional that Monsignor Nebdal commanded her to leave the chambers immediately and denied her observer status on the following days.

In the Hotel Colosseo bar that evening, Sebastian told her that during the afternoon session the questions became more trivial and sometimes outright silly. The interrogators were absolutely convinced that he and Benoir were lovers, though Sebastian repeated that nothing could be farther from the truth. The truth was that Benoir was dedicated ladies man, who surrounded himself with attractive, unmarried women, not to seduce but to continuously test his vow of celibacy.

On the second day, Gabby decided to stand vigil outside the conference room. During a break, a papal clerk approached her to inquire if she would be willing to accompany him to meet a concerned Church official. Her mind flooded with possibilities. Were Vatican plenipotentiaries going to apologize for sending Bosnian hooligans to eliminate her? Was it possible they'd allow her to exhibit the *Yeshu* Fragment in the Shrine of the Book, or would they attempt to punish her for supporting Father Sebastian? There appeared to be no threat in the invitation. Reluctantly, she abandoned her post and followed the clerk through a series of hallways, down a private stairwell, through a small English garden and into an adjacent building, then up another set of stairs to an antechamber.

The clerk instructed, "Please be seated and wait to be summoned."

Itamar had often spoken about his unpleasant battles with the Pope's Secretary of State Donaldo Cardinal Fornenti. Was this power-ful man behind the throne intending to lambast her for her role in the *Yeshu* affair? Or accuse her for leaking it on YouTube?

She was utterly overwhelmed when after four minutes the chamber door opened and standing in the doorway was none other than the Jorge Mario Bergoglio, Pope Francis himself. The diminutive little man didn't dress like a pope or even address her like one. In a simple white robe and small white skullcap, he stepped back to politely allow her passage before him, saying, in stiffly accented English, "Ah hah, my very good Rabbi Lewyn. I've been following your career since your work with Professor Matternly and Father Benoir Matteau. A most remarkable woman, I dare say. Please come in, sit down beside me and we shall have some coffee together. You do drink coffee, don't you?"

Gabby's heart was pounding and for the first time in memory she had having trouble catching her breath. Her opening words got scram-bled in her throat. Here she found herself in the presence the most important religious leader in the world, someone in whose office she had never given credence, someone who led a universal community that had long been in opposition to her own, yet to the faithful the most important leader in the world, and yet in his presence she could barely marshal a response. She swallowed saliva and said, "No…no, sir. Tea if you please."

An ingratiating smile enlarged his baby-faced countenance, "Well then, it must be tea for the good rabbi."

When she managed to collect herself, they chatted amiably about the weather and about Father Sebastian until tea and coffee were placed before them on a silver tray. Gabby thought that perhaps in her feminine role she should pour, but Francis leaned over the table to perform the honors.

"Your lawyers are giving Father Sebastian a rough time in the inquest," Gabby reported once handed a teacup.

"My zealots, of course. In their ardor to protect the Church they are known to be quite rude. I've told them such rudeness is unnecessary, but living entirely within the confines of the Holy See they do not perceive how others see them. Sometimes I think they're envious of our priests who actually perform God's work in their distant parishes, especially the scholarly ones like Father Sebastian Alejandro."

Francis paused in his monologue to take a noisy sip from the rim of his coffee cup. "I know you have come to Rome to support your colleague, but please don't be offended when we ask him to fill in our knowledge about the *Yeshu* Fragment. You see, I'm quite aware of Father Sebastian's career. A fine priest who knows far more about this fragment than of our Curia scholars. And despite what my zealots believe, he's done well for the Church. By reporting on the life of Father Benoir, who incidentally I met once when he was staying or, according to the Israel police, taking refuge in the Vatican."

Gabby added, "In Sebastian's notes he explains how Father Benoir and I were not friends. I supported the position of my boyfriend, Timothy Matternly, and Father Benoir most certainly did not."

"So I'm told. Now that the world knows about the fragment we in the Church must face a new reality. And please don't worry about Father Sebastian. If my zealots treat him rudely, think of it as testing his mettle. If an honest priest won't stand firmly to the historic facts, nobody else will. And we'll all slip back into the darkness that preceded the *Yeshu* Fragment."

Gabby was amazed how openly Francis dealt with the controversial matter. She could only conclude that the Church was now prepared to recognize the authenticity of the YouTube posting.

"Rabbi Lewyn," said the Pope, "when I learned that you had come here to support Father Sebastian, I thought it a good time for us to meet. Since I was elected to this office, I've wanted to end enmity between your people and the Church. It's clear to me, if not to others, that we disagree about the Divinity of Jesus. Your people are a stubborn people who are constitutionally unable to change and that, I believe, is your strength. If we Christians believe that God acts through history, then the fact that your people have endured through impossible trials, by the way many caused by my own Church, is ample proof of Divine favor towards you. You Jews are the trunk of God's tree; we Christians, the branches."

Gabby hardly knew what to say and while she was trying to think of something appropriate the Pope continued, "It is time to end friction between us. There's plenty of room on our planet for differing points of view."

"Even about the *Yeshu* Fragment?" Gabby interrupted.

He had to think about that for a second before saying, "Especially about this fragment. Yes, I believe so. There's no purpose obfuscating facts dealing with the origins of our faith. Faith becomes stronger when tested. Let history speak for itself."

"Your Holiness should know that I didn't leak the fragment to You-Tube. It would please me to know that you accept my word on that."

"Of course I know. And what's also true is that I've always known you didn't do it."

"How does your Eminence know that?"

Pope Francis permitted a wide, expansive smile to enlarge his cheeks. Silence had a way of talking for him. You could say his followers and admirers read into this silence what they wanted. He dropped his head and peered at Gabby over the rims of simple round lenses. She thought she perceived an acknowledging dip of his chin.

Never in her life had she believed that someday she would be in the presence of a Divine Spirit. Perhaps some rabbis believed it possible to stand in the Holy Fire and see the Face of the Lord, but she never did.

In that still moment she understood how she had searched for the leaker in the wrong place. Suddenly there was no doubt in her mind who had done it.

Actually, the most logical person of all!

* * * * *

In Tuscany, Itamar and Gabby began rebuilding the broken road that had separated them. A major ingredient to a fresh start was a dose of wisdom. Neither pried into the secrets of the other. Itamar never learned about Gabby's rape at Wadi Qelt and Gabby never learned exactly what happened on a fateful night between Kar'ine and Itamar in Istanbul. As time passed such events no longer meant much.

Another thing Gabby decided to keep to herself. She loved her people and the faith that had molded them through the centuries. But when she had left the presence of Pope Francis, there was a very brief moment when she felt herself to be Catholic. She knew it wouldn't last and it didn't. But that doesn't mean she couldn't bridge the gap between Judaism and Christianity for an instant.

After all, she argued to herself, when *Yeshu*, the son of Joseph, studied in the school at Ein Arugot there was no difference between Judaism and Christianity. The Roman Church only came on the historic stage three-hundred years later. But like the Jewish people who had endured through the ages, so had the Church.